bottling it up

JOHN P. ROONEY

THE
BLACKSTAFF
PRESS

BELFAST

First published in 2003 by
Blackstaff Press Limited
4c Heron Wharf, Sydenham Business Park
Belfast BT3 9LE
with the assistance of
the Arts Council of Northern Ireland

ARTS
COUNCIL
of Northern Ireland

John P. Rooney has asserted his right under the
Copyright, Designs and Patents Act 1988
to be identified as the author of this work.

Typeset by Techniset Typesetters, Newtown-le-Willows, Merseyside

Printed in Ireland by ColourBooks Limited

A CIP catalogue record for this book is available from the British Library

ISBN 0–85640–743–7

www.blackstaffpress.com

This is a work of fiction. All characters and events portrayed in this
work are fictional. Any resemblance to real people
or incidents is purely coincidental.

JOHN P. ROONEY was born in Belfast and has lived there all his life, apart from four years when he resided variously in Australia, London and Dublin. He has worked in architectural offices in all of these places. While he has written for stage and radio, radio drama has been his forte with over twenty productions to date, one of which won a Giles Cooper award.

for my family

I

Her body heat met his.

She squirmed closer, a wisp of hair brushing his cheek. The strained breathing, her scent, the soft rasping of tights as her knees moved against each other. His body responded like a meerkat scanning the horizon for possibilities. He was lethal. A coiled spring of sexual energy. Just finished his morning run. Showered and shaved. He felt terrific. She pressed closer still. Steady, boy. She was maybe twenty years younger – but so what? The lure of the older man. In the tense silence, her lips drew moistly apart.

'Ever had your blood pressure checked, Mr Fox?'

Looking back, he could see that everything that happened – the clubhouse fire, the dead brickie – sprang from that question. Yet then it hardly registered; hearing was the least employed of his senses. She was a dim outline behind the beam of light as it bored and probed, moving in slow circles around his glaring, bulging eyeball. At last she drew back, no longer a woman but an optician.

'Sorry?'

'Your blood pressure. Ever had it checked?'

He was only there for an eye test!

She swivelled away to her desk and started writing.

'Well, I suggest you see your doctor and have it done right away.'

Doctor? In thirty years he'd been to a doctor only once, and that was for a signature on a passport application. He didn't approve of doctors. Doctors meant illness. He hated illness. He was never ill.

'Something wrong?' He heard his voice rise an octave.

'Oh, nothing really to worry about, Mr Fox.'

There was!

'What?'

She was busy arranging lenses in a box. The reply was tossed over her shoulder: 'Just some nipping veins at the back of the eyes.'

His mouth went dry.

'Nipp –'

'Arteriosclerosis,' she said.

'Arteri –'

'Might be just your time of life.'

Time of life? He was only forty-five!

The meerkat was now down on all fours. And burrowing.

'Can be a sign of raised blood pressure.' Turning round, she saw the panic in his eyes. 'Or it might be nothing. Anyway, no harm to check.'

Smiling, she handed him his new lens prescription. 'Not much change. No deterioration there.'

Your teeth are fine but your gums will have to come out!

She kept smiling at him. But it wasn't the smile of the sex kitten of his fantasy; it was the smile of an Eskimo measuring up the old folks for an ice floe.

He stepped out onto the street. Doddered, really. He was weak, his legs unsteady. He felt suddenly old. Blood pressure! Him! For the first time in his life, he was aware of the blood surging around his body, drumming in his ears, pulsing and pounding like the engine rods on the *Titanic*.

Twenty minutes ago he strode into that place a god; he crept out a hundred-year-old man.

But not for long. Driving back to the office, he thought about things. He began to feel better. A lot better. A hell of a lot better, so much so that he started to smile. Then laugh. For God's sake, what an eejit he'd been, letting himself get worked up like that! After all, her own words: 'might be nothing'! Of course it was nothing; never felt fitter in his life. Fit as a butcher's dog. Three times a week he thrashed Rory at squash – and Rory was ten years younger. And he'd a game that very afternoon, and he'd do the same again. The thought of Rory's red-faced struggles to beat him cheered him up. Doctor indeed! He'd see no friggin doctor. Doctors were for sick people.

'Geronimo!'

He burst into the drawing office in his usual way, vaulting over the secretary's desk, scaring the hell out of poor Valerie. He liked that. Bit of a bastard that way. But he knew she didn't mind; he reckoned she'd a bit of a thing about him. He enjoyed the look on her face as he sailed within inches of her head. She'd nothing to worry about, his reflexes were perfectly tuned. He was a man at the peak of condition, his body a well-oiled machine. Yes, he'd play the game of his life today. He could feel every muscle and sinew throbbing with life and energy. Called him an old man last week had Rory. He'd pay for that. And how! He'd bloody show him there was lead in his pencil yet.

He straightened up, tugged his shirt and jacket back into shape, and scanned the room for his quarry.

'Rory in hiding?' He smirked.

'Paul . . .' squeaked Valerie.

'Don't tell me the shit's cried off. He knows I'm gonna take the knickers off him today!'

No sign. Strange. Rory was always first in. Chickened out, the bastard.

Valerie made another squeaky sound behind him.

'What?'

He looked down at her well-scrubbed, unlipsticked, saved-by-Jesus face. Sad case really, Valerie: no tits, no bum, no personality, doomed to rejoin her maker after a lifetime of virginal spinsterhood. Returned unopened. He was hardly flattered by her admiration. Still, a cat can look at a king. She stared up at him big-eyed. Her lower lip started to wobble. Christ, she was going to blub! Better go easy with his jumping in future.

'Hey, what's up, Val?'

'Didn't . . . you . . . hear?'

'Hear what?'

Her lip wobbled even more. But no words came.

'What?'

'Rory dropped dead last night.'

He felt out of place in the doctor's waiting room. For starters it was full of sick people: old women hawking and spluttering, girls with puking babies, solemn middle-aged women with mysterious middle-aged complaints. He was the only healthy one there. He was the only man there! Ever, probably. And it showed: only women's magazines. And the display leaflets didn't do much for him either: CYSTITIS, THE MENOPAUSE, HAVING A BABY, SMEAR-TESTING, THE WELL-WOMAN CLINIC, BREAST EXAMINATION, FOLIC ACID: WHAT WOMEN SHOULD KNOW. But men weren't totally ignored. Poking out coyly from behind FEELING SUICIDAL? was PROSTATE PROBLEMS. He dribbled the time away with that while trying to shut out the garrulous world of women around him.

'A gorgeous wee girl she had! Seven pound. Y'cud just eat 'er.'

'Och, lovely! An' is he happy?'

'Him! She'd no sooner the stitches out than he's inside again!'

'The dirty brute!'

'Six months he got this time.'

'Oh . . . I thought . . .'

They cackled and slapped each other's knees.

He felt an intruder. He felt they were all looking at him, wondering why a man so obviously in peak condition was there, wasting the doctor's time. He was beginning to wonder himself. The panic that made him grab the first available appointment had subsided somewhat. Poor Rory! A hell of a shock, right enough. Heart attack. Who'd have thought it, and him a non-smoking, non-drinking vegetarian? Never even bothered with women. An icon of clean – if boring – living. And the wake was in character. Who'd ever heard of a vegetarian wake! Really depressed him, that. No drink, carrot juice and veggie sandwiches, and lots of thin, ill-looking people. And then there was Rory lying there. Jesus! One thing to be said for meat eaters: they make lovely corpses. He thought of his own father, a great red beefy glow off him as he lay stretched out in his good suit in his coffin, like he'd just come in from a walk on a blustery day. Not like Rory. Poor Rory, luminously green – a pea returned to its pod.

'Mr Fox?'

The doctor peered round his door, calling out to the crowded room. Paul stood up and the doctor nodded him over. He followed him into the room. A weedy type, the doctor, no shoulders, shallow chest, legs like matchsticks. Never make a rugby player. Seen more meat on a fork. Wouldn't even make a corner flag.

The tiny surgery closed in on him; not designed for a big man. He was unsure of the etiquette of such places. As he entered, the doctor was already at his desk, scribbling. Should he stand or sit, talk or remain silent? Like being back in school. While he awaited direction, his eye toured the cluttered room. On the wall above the desk was a large picture of a plate overflowing with three fried eggs, four sausages, three rashers of bacon, two pieces of fried bread, three pieces of fried potato bread, three pieces of black pudding. The plate had a black rim. Below was the caption: WELCOME TO BELFAST – HEART ATTACK CAPITAL OF THE WORLD.

'Right!' The doctor swung round.

Paul jumped.

'What's the problem?'

This was a seriously busy man. He thought of the tide of snuffling humanity outside awaiting its turn. He felt almost apologetic.

'Hello, doctor. I don't think we've actually met before. I never –'

'The problem?'

'Pardon?'

'What's wrong with you?'

Not one for small talk.

'Well, I was having my eyes tested –'

Immediately the doctor was on his feet, hauling over a piece of equipment to where Paul stood.

'Blood pressure,' he said. 'Sit down please and roll up your sleeve!'

How did he know?

The doctor saw the look on his face.

'It's how most cases are picked up. No symptoms, see . . . That is, till you drop dead.' He laughed and looked encouragingly at Paul's shocked face.

It wasn't a laughing matter.

'Surprisingly common. One in five people over forty

have high blood pressure and hardly any of them know it.'
He stared intently at the gauge as he pumped air into the
cloth band around Paul's arm.

The blood pounded against the tightening restriction.
Paul's veins bulged. When he felt his arm would explode,
the pressure was suddenly released with a sigh of escaping air.

'Mmm.' The doctor studied the gauge for a bit. He
repeated the operation, then tidied away the equipment.

Paul waited for the verdict.

'Did you walk here?' said the doctor.

'I drove.'

'Mmmm ...'

'Why?'

'Would've accounted for it.'

Accounted for what?

'Exercise can put it up,' said the doctor.

Paul didn't like what he was hearing.

'So ... 190 over 95,' mused the doctor.

'Is that bad?'

The doctor looked thoughtful. 'It's OK ...'

Paul relaxed.

'... for a hundred-year-old man!'

His stomach tightened.

'Query heart disease,' said the doctor.

'You serious!'

The doctor drew back. His seriousness was rarely
questioned.

'Other possibility is I excite you a lot.' He laughed.
Heartily.

Query arse bandit!

Then the engine rods again. This was scary stuff. He was
entering uncharted territory. Fitness-wise he'd always been
up to the mark, and beyond. But now – this. Heart disease!
He didn't quite know what it meant, but he felt a shadow

had fallen across his life. It had to be faced: he'd joined the ranks of the unwell. He hated the unwell. Now he was one of them, doomed forever to clutter up chemists' shops, doctors' waiting rooms, operating theatres. He was one of the losers, a beaten docket thrown on the bookie's floor of life. It all stretched before him: bad health, unemployment, poverty. Death. It was bad enough heading for fifty on a runaway Exocet; now this! A doleful awareness of his mortality shrouded him. The finiteness of it all. The biblical span. For him – if he lasted – only twenty-five more summer holidays, twenty-five Christmases, twenty-five Triple Crowns, twenty-five rides (Mary had made plain that once a year was quite enough for her, thank you very much).

The doctor saw his alarm. 'Not to worry. The white-coat effect can put it up.'

He wasn't wearing a white coat.

The doctor sat thinking for a moment. 'Look, we'll not do anything today . . .'

Paul stiffened. Bypass operation? Transplant? Surely he'd be given notice of something like that!

'Do you smoke?'

'No, thanks.'

'I wasn't offering.'

'Oh.'

'Drink?'

'Moderately.'

'How much, say, in a week?'

'Mmm . . . maybe twenty pints.'

Mostly all in one go on Fridays. But he didn't add that.

The failure of the usual suspects disappointed the doctor. He eyed Paul's physique.

'I can see you're fit.'

'As a butcher's dog.'

'Pardon?'

'Never fitter.'

'Any family history of high blood pressure?'

'No.'

'Mmmm ...' He leaned closer. 'Is there ... is there anything ... y'know ... on your mind?'

'Pardon?'

'Stress can put it up.' Again the 'tell me all' look. 'Anything worrying you?'

'Only my blood pressure.'

He smiled. The doctor didn't.

'Anything else?'

He could have told him about Mary and the separation. But there was no point. No children involved. He couldn't honestly say it was stressing him. If anything, a part of him was quite looking forward to the single state again. A private part.

'Nothing.'

The doctor held his gaze, as if sizing him up. He tilted his head as a new thought struck.

'Could be a personality thing,' he said.

Ah, no! None of this head-shrinker stuff, please! Mary's territory, that. She had dozens of books about it, all mostly American paperbacks with sad-looking women on the cover with black clouds over their heads. Her latest was *The Little Book of Calm*. It was the one book that really put him in a rage. Not that he'd ever read it, but he knew the types who had. Dickheads.

'You're familiar with the concept of Type-A and B personalities?'

There was no shaking him off.

'I'd take you for a B. You bottle up feelings instead of letting them out. Am I close?'

Close-ish. Frig him.

'Look, doctor ...'

'The typical Alpha man shouts and roars and kicks ass. Healthier all round. One of life's little unfairnesses again – the evil bastards live longer. A scientific fact.'

Paul had always fancied himself an ass-kicker. Now he'd been outed. He was only a B in an A's clothing.

'I don't think . . .'

But the doctor had already disengaged, swinging back to his desk, reaching for a syringe.

'Or maybe it's nothing at all. Just a fluke reading. Happens.'

That's what Paul wanted to hear.

Turning back, he exposed Paul's bare forearm.

'I'll just take some blood, check your cholesterol count. You might feel a bit of a sting . . .'

He closed his eyes as the needle went in. He wasn't good with pain. God, what must it be like having a baby! At least Mary'd been spared that.

As soon as he was done, the doctor was on his feet, shepherding him towards the door. He couldn't have been in more than seven minutes.

'Make another appointment – say, two weeks' time – and I'll test you again.'

'Thanks, doctor.'

And he meant it. 'A fluke.' He treasured the word. Of course it was a fluke.

The doctor stopped him in the doorway. 'Y'know, I'd say if it's anything, it's stress.'

Paul attempted a chuckle. 'Stress . . . me? I don't think so, doctor.'

'Nothing wrong with stress. It's how you handle it. Don't bottle things up! Be an evil bastard and live!'

'Yes, doctor,' he said.

And again, at the door, 'Remember . . . Don't bottle it up!'

Tense! Him? The waiting patients jumped at the sound of him pulling the door behind him.

OK, at times he was a bit worked up. Who wasn't! But stress? He prided himself on dealing with anything life threw at him. Nerves of steel, him. Stress was for big girls' blouses. Everybody knew that.

Or so he pretended. But that was his public face. In reality he was a daylight macho-man; only at night and to himself would he admit the inadmissible. Of course his life was stressful. Wasn't everybody's? Just part of living. And his was especially so with Mary. Rows all the time. Rows about him going away on rugby weekends. Rows about coming back at all hours from the pub. Rows about finding lipstick on his shirts. Rows about rows. But it was now all in the past. Since the separation, there'd been a great peace.

Hadn't been his idea to split up. No way. He didn't want to leave the house; all his stuff was there – and his memories. And the thing was, he didn't actually dislike Mary. Not really. It was more her attitude to things, to him. She seemed to have given up on so much: even on trying to make the most of herself, how she looked, how she dressed. And she sneered at those who did. 'Bimbos,' she said, and 'Tarts'. Compared to the other men's wives in the rugby club, she looked ten years older. 'Mutton dressed as lamb,' she'd say about them. And if he happened to make some helpful suggestion, hoping to improve her appearance, she'd take it as a challenge. 'Well, this is what you married!' she'd say. But she was wrong. He'd married a beautiful, vibrant, twenty-five-year-old girl. Where had she gone?

But he couldn't really blame her wanting him to leave. He could be a bit of a shit at times. He wasn't the easiest to live with, he knew that. But nobody's perfect. Lucky they never had kids – Mary's banjaxed womb – breaking up would be so much worse. They were spared that. No, things were much better now on his own. And for her too, he supposed. Stress was eased all round.

Except for his job. Now there was stress. And some. After twenty years' service as a council architect, he was reduced virtually to the role of a maintenance man. All the interesting new-build work was being given out to housing associations. The councils were left with the dregs: rehabilitation of older housing stock with tenants *in situ*. A nightmare. Ken, his team leader, said the glory days of public housing were over, they'd just have to swallow their pride. But it was rubbish work.

The estate he was to visit that day was typical. He wasn't looking forward to it.

2

Le Corbusier had said that a house is a machine for living in. If that was so, 7 Prince Charles Mews was ready for the breaker's yard. Paul eyed it from a safe distance. An early example of the council house 'Good-Enough-for-Them' school of architecture, it had lived down to its expectations with a relish. His job: do something with it. He took a deep breath, dragged the broken gate aside and started up the path.

The house wasn't nearly as nice as it looked. The front door had that lived-in appearance *de rigueur* for the estate: smashed glass with cardboard backing; scuffed timber bottom panel embellished with boot prints and urine stains – animal and human; a hole where there had been a letter box; and all surmounting a tide of cigarette packets, poly-styrene carry-out containers and crisp bags, washing up against the step. A plastic number 7 dangled unluckily from a nail.

There was, however, a welcome on the mat.

''S fuckin open!'

From deep inside, the shouted invitation answered his knock. Good start. The chances of getting tenants – or, in housing management speak 'customers' – up before noon weren't great.

The door scraped across the linoleum as he pushed his way in.

The customer's introduction was short on formality.

'Tell yeh I'm a sex offender, did they?'

It was more accusation than question. Paul hovered about the living-room entrance, his back pressed tight against the wall. Could be an arse bandit for all he knew. They hadn't told him about this one.

The man was watching TV in his underpants and eating a fried-egg sandwich off a plate on his knee. He wasn't happy having his breakfast disturbed.

'I'll be quick,' Paul said, evading the question. 'Just a few measurements.'

He would be quick. And how. Entering the house, he'd nearly gagged at the heady cocktail of sights and smells that greeted him. A fumigation job, this one. He wanted to cover his mouth and nose with his scarf, but he resisted. Never give customers the impression that you're looking down on them, management had said. Be customer-friendly, they'd said.

And he was. Ever so. To save the man's blushes, he attempted a cheery professional indifference.

'Bad weather we're having!'

It didn't work. And the man didn't blush.

'Shithouse, init?' He flung out a tattooed arm at the squalor around him. 'Don't get many callers, see. All know about me round here. Even the Lodge's friggin fucked me out.'

Paul twitched. To him, Orangemen were like Islamic fundamentalists – but without their sense of fun. Normally he gave them a wide berth. Still, as a public servant he'd to deal with all sorts without fear or favour.

He smiled.

He really hated this work. He hated having to be nice to arseholes; hated having to appear interested in patching up their grubby homes. He'd a first-class honours degree in architecture, for God's sake! He hadn't spent seven years at university to be a glorified maintenance man! Ken said they should all be glad they still had a job, they were closing down council architects' departments all over. Anyway, Ken said Paul would soon have a decent new-build contract starting; a plumb job too, one Ken would normally have kept for himself. It was a huge new phase of five hundred houses, an extension to an existing site which was now at plastering-out stage. But this wasn't out of the goodness of his heart; Ken didn't operate like that. No, it was on the wrong side of the peace line. 'Horses for courses,' Ken had said. Step forward Seamus O'Catholic! Still, it suited. Now he could do the work he was trained for. No more of this stuff. The jail door was opening.

'Interfered wi' nobody, me.'

Paul dodged his eye.

'I'm no prevert.'

This as Paul was at full stretch, reaching for the ceiling with the tape.

'Well ... not as what you'd call a prevert. Not inteferin wi' women and childer – disgustin that is. None o' that, like.'

Just then Paul felt a warm caress below his waistline. He leaped as if electrocuted.

'Jesus!'

A large Dobermann pinscher, sleek as a seal, had padded unnoticed into the room. It planted its nose companionably in Paul's crotch. The brown eyes locked onto his. A low growl did for introduction.

The man swivelled his eyes from the screen, pieces of partly masticated egg jiggling from his chin. A half-smile disgorged more detritus.

''Snot everybody she takes to, y'know.'

'Grrrrr.'

Paul moved back. The nose followed.

'She safe?'

'Grrrrrr.'

'Long as I'm here . . .'

'Grrrrr.'

'Electric metre man came in one time I was out – dog nearly had the leg off 'im at the arse.'

He reached across and caressed its back.

'Normally, like, wouldn't hurt a fly. All lies what they say, girl. Init, girl?' He smiled into the dog's eyes like a lover.

'Grrrrr.'

'Just likes to nose people a bit.'

Paul had a terror of dogs. Even its nose looked sharp. A perfectly rational fear, he reckoned: dogs didn't fight fair – they knew he wouldn't bite back.

'Would you put her in another room, please?'

'Can't.'

'Why?'

'Chew through the bloody door, she would!'

'Outside on the street, then?'

'Hates strangers.'

Paul remained motionless, transfixed on the dog's nose.

'Look, I can't work like this.'

The nose became more insistent.

'See . . . just wants to give you a bit of a nuzzle.'

The man leaned back, eyes dimming with a dreamy faraway look. 'Beautiful shape, in't she? Beautiful.' Then quickly, 'For a dog, like.'

Paul had a sudden horrible inkling of what the man's offence might be.

'Anyway, about this kip . . .' He put down the sandwich and assumed as businesslike a manner as a man wearing only underpants could. 'When's this first phrase gonna start, then?'

Paul relaxed. Normal conversation at last.

'Latest info is it's been delayed six months,' he announced, regaining his bright, detached, professional manner.

'Wha . . .' The man had stopped eating. His mouth hung open.

Further explanation obviously required.

'Budget cuts.'

The man seemed to struggle for air. 'Fuck! Fuck!'

The look of pure hatred alarmed Paul.

'Y'mean . . . y'mean I'm gonna be here another six months!'

A bit of defusing called for.

'But anyway, you're in phase two, aren't you?' he consoled.

The man's eyes bulged. Paul stepped back.

'Phrase two? Phrase two? Aw, fuck off . . . I was told phrase one!'

Each time he said 'phrase' an angry spray of crumbs and spit showered the room.

Things were turning ugly.

In his indignation, the man stood up, tipping plate and food remnants to the floor. The dog was onto it.

Paul saw his chance and sidled past the snaffling hound out of the room. The man followed.

'Phrase fuckin one I was told!'

Down the hall and out into the garden. The dog now joining the chase.

'Your area's been reclassified as phase two,' Paul panted over his shoulder, 'and phase two is now phase one.'

Still the man came on. The pursuit dogged. He lit up with a joyous revelation. 'Ah ha, I know . . . I fuckin know! It's all them fenians in phrase two gettin eveythin that's goin! Am't I right? Ay? Ay?'

The dog reappeared between its master's legs. They made a handsome couple.

Paul quickened his pace out onto the street. The man stood in his garden, shouting after him.

'Hey, you! C'mere, you, back! I haven't fuckin finished!'

Paul kept going.

'Yous are a parcel of fuckin useless wankers in that fuckin council! Yous fuck up fuckin everythin!'

Such an intellectual thrashing demanded a riposte – but he remembered he was a public servant.

The man remembered also.

'Hey, an don't forget . . . I'm payin your fuckin wages!'

Paul paused and looked back at his half-naked, unemployed, serial benefits-claiming benefactor.

'Any chance of a rise, then?' he said.

A hurricane of fucks followed him into his car.

Normally he would have left it at that: a token drawing of blood, not enough to give the tenant grounds for a complaint – the customer is always right, after all. But today he needed more. He felt the blood pounding in his ears. He needed release. Don't bottle it up, the doctor said. As he moved off, he hesitated for a bit – then slowly, deliberately, obscenely, in full view of the still-cursing yet highly esteemed customer, he gave the two fingers out of the side window.

It was the start.

Driving back to the office, his knuckles were white on the steering wheel. Never noticed that before. Stress! Was it always like that? Site supervision wasn't for the faint-hearted. Good ones were born, not made. The estates he worked in were fast becoming sink estates where problem tenants were dumped and allowed to fester. Attempts at integrating such people into stable communities had long since been abandoned, leaving the social services and people like himself to pick up the pieces. He could think of better ways to spend his day.

Dealing with awkward tenants in various states of sobriety took its toll. Essential attributes were a screwed-on smile, no sense of smell, a touch of deafness and the sensitivity of an elephant's scrotum. Delicacy of feeling was reserved for the sad, skinny cats and dogs that slunk about the place. But for other life forms any hint of weakness was fatal. And once they'd tasted blood . . .

The council-issue anorak didn't help matters either: bright yellow with the circular council logo emblazoned on the back like a target, ideal for being stalked by irate tenants. It was open season on the wearer. It drew them like a bitch on heat. Even the lowliest human derelict – the local wino who burnt his own floorboards for fuel – felt he owned a piece of the man from the council. Like all the other architects, he dreaded walking about the estates. It was open country with no cover. He was the sick wildebeest hobbling along at the back of the herd with the lions closing in. They'd coined a phrase for the condition: Anoraksia nervosa.

Starting to get him down, it was. You could take only so much of this stuff: vermin-infested houses, Giro-drop addresses, houses being used as massage parlours, drinking dens, shooting gallerys, public toilets. Then there were the beaten wives, drunken husbands, live-in lovers, Rottweiler breeders, multiple cat lovers, squatters, religious maniacs, unfrocked priests, madmen, sad men, wanted men, gunmen, chancers, dole fiddlers, rent defaulters, sex offenders – and that was only this morning's round.

It wasn't that he didn't care; he did. But familiarity was killing his compassion. The brotherhood of man, for whom the bell tolls and all that – he was all for that! Trouble was, he'd found the bell tolls louder for some than for others. And in Prince Charles Mews the tolling was definitely muted. It was a jingle out there!

The entrance wall to the estate had painted on it in

two-foot-high letters ONE FAITH, ONE CROWN. NO POPE IN OUR TOWN. Tourists took photos; catholics took the hint. And life was no easier for the builders who had to work in these places. On top of everything else they had to deal with the local protection racketeers who masqueraded as criminals but deep down were really something much worse: patriots. What they said went. Their every whim had to be catered to.

And it was a whim of iron.

3

A quarter to ten!

Trouble. He'd arranged to have his leg broken at half nine – and he was late.

Half nine, they'd said; half nine sharp. Knee-cappings were generally later, when things were quiet, but leg breaking was always at half nine; everybody knew that. And these people weren't the sort you kept waiting. He hoped there wasn't a queue. He was really annoyed with himself. He prided himself on punctuality.

His pace quickened, but the drink was slowing him down. Not used to whiskey. He scurried on through the back alleyways, clattering into upturned rubbish bins, past broken-down timber fences, discarded pushchairs, yapping dogs.

The friggin pub. He was too long in the pub. Didn't want to leave. Hoping for something, anything – a miracle. There was none. Drink was his only comforter. The idea was to get a few down – wouldn't feel it the same, they said – but not so many you couldn't show. Trick was getting the balance right. He'd read about ones who didn't show.

'What t'fuck kept yeh?'

They were waiting behind the shops. Six of them. All masked. Two with baseball bats.

'We thought you'd done a runner.'

'Or touted to the peelers.'

'More sense, though, hadn't you, lad?' This one's voice was soft. Kindly even.

'Miserable lookin shite, in't he, Mary?'

The kindly one swung round and smacked the speaker's face. Hard. The man stumbled back.

'What t'fuck did I say! What'd I say about names – specially that name?'

The man rubbed his jaw. 'Forgot.'

'You'll friggin remember next time.'

They turned to the matter in hand. Two of them took him by the shoulders and lowered him to the ground. He didn't resist. A fag was offered. His fingers couldn't hold it. Then he remembered he'd forgotten to put on clean under-wear. Too late now.

'Glad you didn't do a runner, ay? Least this way you'll wake up tomorra.'

They laughed.

The kindly one was looking down at him.

'Been a bad boy, haven't we? Antisocial activities! What's it say in yer catechism, lad? "Thou shall not fuckin well steal." Right? See what happens when you go agin yer catechism!'

The baseball bats took a last drag and flicked their butts off into the darkness. Down to business. They adjusted their grips and shuffled their feet, like golfers preparing to tee off.

A rag was tied round his mouth.

'Left or right?'

They looked at the kindly one. He considered the matter. 'Left.'

Four men, each holding an arm or a leg, now pinioned him to the cold ground. He was limp, resigned, wanting it over. A breezeblock was pushed under his left calf.

For a moment the kindly one surveyed his handiwork.

'On second thoughts . . .'

The baseball bats looked up.

'On second thoughts . . .'

The kindly one grunted as he bent down again and this time pushed a breezeblock under the right calf as well. At this his victim convulsed in a violent struggle.

The kindly one looked hurt.

'Fair play now, lad! You were late, remember?'

The others sniggered.

Gently, like a mother undressing her child, he bent down again and rolled up each trouser leg, baring the startling whiteness.

'There now!'

The legs jerked and writhed, pulling and bucking against their restraints.

'There now. All be over in a tick, lad.'

The kindly one grunted as he straightened up. He gave the nod.

A strangled scream escaped the gag. From his prone position, he saw the clubs rise high into the glare of the street-lamps.

He shut his eyes. Money was stuffed into his top pocket.

'Yer taxi to the hospital, lad.'

Nice touch, he thought.

4

The leg breaking didn't even make the news. Paul only heard about it because it happened at the back of his site and kids were collecting splinters of bone as souvenirs – time off from robbing old ladies and setting fire to cats. The whole business depressed him. It was symptomatic. This town was going down the toilet, fast. Nowadays this was mere run-of-the-mill stuff; it was just how disputes were settled. Broken legs, smashed kneecaps ... whatever happened to solicitors' letters, for Christ's sake!

Recently he'd been avoiding going out to site. The aggro, the stress – who needed it? Especially now, when he might have his blood pressure to watch. He'd need a horse tranquilliser before he could set foot in 7 Prince Charles Mews again. No, life in the office was more appealing: the calm, the bantering, the grumbling companionship of the disaffected. Here he was no longer the hunted. Here he was among his own.

And there was Joan, beautiful Joan from housing management. He'd never spoken to her, but he fantasised a lot. Joan with her short skirts and voluptuous figure was the stuff of dreams. Mary had looked like that once. In the early days. A long time ago. But Joan was here and now – a lit match in a testosterone-fuelled petrol tank. All work stopped when she came into view. And as she passed, male yearning vibrated in her highly scented wake. She was a walking orgasm. She was in her early thirties and – he had made a point of finding out – divorced. Openings for willing lads.

He'd caught her eye once or twice – not a lot to go on, admittedly, but an achievement nonetheless. Housing management people didn't speak much to the architects. They considered themselves a higher life form, above such mundane mechanical activities as designing and building houses. They were management; their work was much more important and all-encompassing. In the eyes of housing management, the architects were merely a technical resource to be called upon when needed, the factory equivalent of shop-floor workers on the tools. In vain would the architects summon up Michelangelo and Bernini in defence of their calling. Unsportingly, management would point to the tower blocks being dynamited down the road. No, there could be no meeting of minds. There was management and there were the technical people, and ne'er the twain shall meet. Genetic engineering had not yet advanced to the stage where mating between housing officers and architects could be envisaged. But Paul had his hopes. And besides, he was a single man again. Almost.

Yes, Joan was one reason to desert the site. But today there was another, less arousing one: a pep talk about their futures, about how they would have to do more in less time or the architects' department would be shut down. Market testing had arrived. This stuff bored him to tears. He had long ago lost interest in office politics. Anyway, there was little point. Everyone knew the technical people were going nowhere. The future belonged to management types with their organisational career maps and sharp elbows. Survival meant keeping out of their way.

He sighed, took out his brain and ascended in the lift to the twelfth floor.

Was it symbolic that Belfast's most famous export sank on its maiden voyage? Paul's mind was a Hoover for such idle speculation. He sat by the window, tapping a pencil between his teeth. Below, the city sulked in an autumn gloaming. It matched his mood. Everything about the place annoyed him today. He dredged up irritations to wallow in. Anything was fodder; anything as long as it distracted him from what was going on in the room before him.

'... To survive, everyone must pull his weight. We must embrace the market concept wholeheartedly. We're all in the one boat. We either swim together or ...'

This *Titanic* thing, he could never really understand it. This pride in supposed local achievement. What achievement? The friggin thing sank, for Christ's sake! Went down like a stone! What worse fate could befall a ship? Anywhere else such an event would be treated like a scandalous relative: mentioned only in whispers between consenting adults. But not here. Here people boasted of grandas who were riveters or whatever on it. Boasted! Christ's sake, they should have been put on a register like child molesters and watched. And there was even talk of making a scale model of it for a floating restaurant on the Lagan no less! But floating for how long, diners would be anxious to know? And was a hard frost expected?

A silence. He cocked an ear.

'Furthermore ...'

False alarm. Steve had mileage in him yet, fuelled as he was with his own self-importance. Paul had little respect for anyone in management and for Steve none at all. Despite his sharp suit and careful grooming, there was a lot less to him than met the eye. In a world of mediocrities he stood head and shoulders below the rest. Even his attempts at ingratiating himself with his superiors were second rate. They had the measure of him. He was only a nodder; never quite made it to a yes man. He had his uses when there was dirty work to be done, but apart from that they took little notice of him. Other than his utter malleability, no one could understand what his qualifications were for this new public relations job. He rose without trace. The Masons were mentioned. He was a renegade architect who had jumped aboard the management life raft at the first hint of market testing; and, as an architect, he made the perfect Judas goat to lead the others to where management wished them to go. A newcomer to market testing, he now burned with the zeal of the convert.

'. . . mission statements . . . goal setting . . . measurement . . . efficiency . . . benchmarking . . .'

There were times Paul really hated this town, his native place, this rock whence he was hewn. Why couldn't he have been hewn from New York, or Paris, or, well, anywhere else really? The thought depressed him even more. His gaze slid over the grey cityscape, taking in the sweep of the hills, the dull gleam of the lough, the giant yellow cranes dwarfing the gantries and the sprawl of sheds and workshops that had once been the biggest shipyard in the world. Right now, in some far-off Siberia of the Irish diaspora, there was sure to be a sad bastard crying into his pint, homesick for all this, dreaming of coming back, coming home. A dog returning to its vomit.

'. . . necessity of hitting targets, control, budget holder, teamworking, motivation . . .'

Paul's head began to droop. The radiator was going full blast beside him. His lids were heavy. In the background the monotone mantra droned on. He was gone.

His mind slid free, untethering itself to browse the sunlit

uplands of his beckoning future. A bright new world awaited him out there: new adventures, new conquests. A single man again. New, young and exciting women to meet. But there was a problem: where to meet such new and exciting women? There were no dances any more such as he'd known in his chasing days. Just discos. He'd watched the queues outside these places. Everyone about fourteen. He'd scouted the singles bars: middle-twenties scene. Even there he'd look like he was hanging around to collect his daughter. The fear of humiliation held him back from such places. He'd even begun looking at the Lonely Hearts column in the *Belfast Telegraph*. Desperation this, but it proved more fruitful territory. The ad jumped out at him right away:

> JANE: WARM, WITTY, INTELLIGENT, MATURE, PROFESSIONAL LADY (P), INTERESTED IN ART, POLITICS, LITERATURE, GOOD CONVERSATION, WOULD LIKE TO MEET SIMILAR-MINDED PROFESSIONAL GENTLEMAN 45–50, NON-SMOKER, WITH GSOH AND OHAC, WITH VIEW TO GIVING AND RECEIVING TLC, FRIENDSHIP, AND WHATEVER MIGHT FOLLOW.

It was 'whatever might follow' that hooked him. He liked the teasing tone of it. Could this be she, his future destiny? Seemed just what he was looking for: someone intelligent, witty and sensitive. Was this his kindred spirit? There could be a hitch, though. While he was confident in his GSOH and TLC, he wasn't sure if he measured up in the OHAC department. Who knows what he'd own after the divorce settlement. Then there was her (P) as against his (RC), but he felt love could make such distinctions irrelevant. Cultivated people like themselves should be above all that. But what did 'mature' mean? Responsible? Past it? Fermenting? It wasn't that he was just after sex; he genuinely wanted a relationship, a companion, someone interesting to talk to and do things with – someone, in fact, like Mary used to be, but without her present shape, attitude or DIY skills. He wanted a womanly woman, mature or not, free from the aroma of dry rot fluid and sawdust. But still, OK, the thought of a young firm body was exciting. But what would they have in common, he and a twenty-year-old? What interests could they share? What would they talk about . . . the latest pop charts? A short conversation, that. Five minutes would be sure to exhaust all possibilities. But of course there was always –

'Hey!'

An elbow in the side jerked him awake. Tony grinned down into his face.

'Watch this,' he whispered, nodding towards the still-talking Steve. He tilted a buttock and began screwing up his face as if in pain.

Paul knew what was coming. Tony was a serious breaker of wind, a master farter, an Olympic contender. Farting was his forte. It wasn't just a matter of noise with him; it was musical arrangement. He was an aesthete of wind. On a good day he could do 'Yankee Doodle' in D. Today, though, he could manage only a three-noter – the key indefinable. A triumph nonetheless.

Gasps of appreciation from those around him.

Steve faltered like a hunted deer hit in mid-stride; but he carried on.

It was Tony's party piece. But not his only one; he was also into farmyard impressions. Farmyard impressions were big with all the architects, almost as popular as farting. Their feral gruntings and honkings to each other across the drawing office, honed to perfection during long, soporific, summer afternoons, were rare outlets for creative impulses in an environment bled dry of intellectual stimulation; an environment where deciding the colour of bathroom tiles could make one's day.

'Accountability –' red-faced and poised for flight, Steve fired his final salvo from the door of the drawing office – 'that's what it's all about! And everyone must cooperate with whatever procedures will be put in place.'

Silence.

Then.

'Mooooo!'

The cows led off. The hens followed, then the pigs, then horses, then a duet of squalling cats, then a speciality of Tony's which he maintained was donkeys humping – all building up to a crazy crescendo.

Steve fled the room. The final barb followed him through the door.

'Dickhead!'

Their tormentor gone, the architects settled back behind their terminals. But uneasily. They tried to dismiss what had just been heard, but a frisson of fear energised the silence. Paul was the first to dispel it.

'What an arsehole!'

They laughed in nervous agreement.

'At least that's got some function,' said Ken.

More laughter.

'You lot are awful ...' Val didn't like unpleasantness. She wanted everybody to be friends. 'You really are!'

Nobody heeded her.

'Him giving us orders! No way! The union'll have something to say about this,' said Tony.

Even Stella was in attack mode. 'God's sake! A year ago that prick was colouring in drawings for me!'

They looked at her. This wasn't the Stella they all knew and loathed. Normally she toadied to anyone in authority;

was famous for it. Steve's recent elevation to market testing public relations officer obviously stung. It was common knowledge that she'd put in for the job. She was a woman scorned.

'*Colouring in my bloody drawings!*' Her voice vibrated with disgust.

'And even making a mess of that!' said Tony in support.

'A dickhead,' said Paul.

'You lot are really, really awful!' Val protested.

'Little rat!' said Stella.

They sniggered.

'Prick!' she added for good measure.

Try as he might, Paul just couldn't take to Stella. He wasn't alone. Her aloofness, her self-centredness kept everyone at a distance. How did her husband stick her for the brief time he did! She was the ice maiden without the looks, the mystery or the maidenhood – just the ice. Nothing seemed to impinge on her until her own interests were involved. But now resentment, Paul noted, made her almost human. He was well aware of her problems, of course. Divorced with two young children, life wasn't easy. Her job meant everything and she took care not to jeopardise it, hence her obsequiousness to authority. Now in her early forties, hopes of remarriage and financial security were fast fading. But even allowing for all that, he just could not take to her. She had an air of thinking herself better than everyone else. She wasn't quite a snob, but she was saving up to be one.

'But remember,' said Val, 'he did do that management course the rest of you scorned.' She always tried to see the best in people.

Ken gave no quarter. 'A brown-nosing job, that!'

'Well, you can't blame him for trying to better himself, can you?' she protested.

Paul looked at her. 'Frig's sake, Val!'

'Well, fair's fair!'

Her refusal to join the general feeding frenzy grated. She was a vegetarian hound in a stag hunt. Everyone needed some hate in them. Some good purging viciousness. Only healthy. What fun was there in being forever understanding?

'All I'm saying is he's just trying to improve himself!'

'With a bit more polish, he could be a rough diamond,' sniggered Paul.

'Sand-blasting, y'mean,' smirked Ken.

Val swung away in a huff.

'Well, he's *management* now, so he is –' Stella spat out the word as much in envy as in scorn – 'and he can rise as high as he likes, unlike the rest of us drones.' She knew that she too had the potential and ambition to rise through the ranks, but then she was technical and that made the difference. She was quite prepared to lick as much arse as Steve, but in the circumscribed world of the technical people there wasn't much influential arse on offer.

'What's it he calls himself now?' Paul injected incredulity into every word. 'Market testing public relations officer! . . . Frig me!'

'Big title for such a wee bollocks.' Stella knew how much more convincingly the title would have rested on her own person.

'Means bugger all, of course,' said Paul.

'And I wouldn't trust him an inch. Stab you in the front, he would,' said Tony.

'Y'mean the back,' said Paul.

Tony shook his head. 'He'd know you'd be expecting it there.'

'He'll make everybody's life a bloody misery,' said Ken.

'If he's let.' As a strong union person, Tony liked to remind people that they weren't alone. He was behind them;

and behind him in turn stood the massed battalions of organised labour.

'And anyway he's common as muck.' It was Stella's killer point.

They looked at her.

Tony shrugged. 'He's a tosser.'

Again there was silence. Only the hum of the terminals and the clicking of keyboards. Then:

'It's the first step, isn't it?' said Stella, her voice now softer, vulnerable almost.

'What?' said Tony.

'This market testing. It's the first step to getting rid of us all.'

'Joan, housing management, here. To whom am I speaking?'

Paul looked quickly round the room. He couldn't believe this. Was somebody taking a hand out of him? No. They were all now gathered around Tony's desk.

It really was her!

All the talk about Steve and office politics was depressing him and he'd just moved over to his own work station when the phone rang.

'Ah ... Paul here.'

He felt his breath catching. God, she really was having an effect on him! This was ridiculous. The old shake was back. A lifetime of marriage dropping away. He was twenty-one again with a few pints aboard and a girl giving him the come-on.

'Oh, hi, Paul ... Paul, I'm the new housing officer for your area. I don't know if you've heard ...'

Was he dreaming?

'I'll be looking after your rehabilitation scheme, Paul, and your new site ...'

She kept using his name, like she'd known him for ever.

He bathed in it. He steadied himself. This was his chance to say something sharp – first impressions were so important – something that would show her that, even if he was only an architect, he was somebody, that he was different from all the other guys she'd ever known; a chance to say something she'd remember for ever; something that would send her oestrogen fizzing.

'Hi!' he said.

'Bit of a crisis, Paul. Hope you can help me.'

A kidney? A bone-marrow transplant?

'What is it?'

'Could you get the builder to stop work immediately on Mr Burke's handicapped extension?'

This was a large handicapped extension tacked onto the rear of a council house – special bedroom, shower, special toilet, concrete ramp to front door, etc. – total cost about twenty grand. Mr Burke, a painter, married with two kids, had fallen off a roof and was paralysed from the waist down. His life was spent in a wheelchair and his council house was being adapted to suit him. Rumour had it that he had just received a huge compensation award.

'They're just putting the final coat of paint on it. What's up?'

Silence.

'You mean it's finished?'

'As good as.'

'Shit!'

That sweet mouth did things for the word.

'Pardon?'

'Oh, sorry, Paul.'

'Something wrong, Joan?'

It was the first time he'd used her name. They'd have to get married now.

'Plenty, I'm afraid. Our paraplegic Mr Burke has just

run off with his district nurse!'

The corner of his mouth twitched.

'You're kidding!'

Again the spasm.

'Just heard this minute.'

It was 'run off' that did it. The mad spasm again.

'Left wife and family. Just buggered off!'

'Shit!' He liked sharing the word with her.

He hoped he sounded suitably indignant. But a manic grin was spreading across his face. He was glad Joan couldn't see him.

'Terrible, isn't it?' she sighed.

'Terrible,' he agreed.

He wanted to roar. Try as he might, the image wouldn't leave him: Mr Burke tearing off in his wheelchair down the street with the district nurse across his knees, scorched rubber marks on his wee mobility ramp the only evidence of his passing.

'Now we're left with this extension and nobody to use it!' she complained.

'Just have to push somebody else off a roof.'

It was out before he was aware of it. One of his smart-aleck remarks best kept to himself.

'Oh, Paul!'

It was an admonition. But behind it there was just a hint of a smile.

'Sorry. Stupid thing to say!'

'Oh, I know what you mean. There's something in all of us makes us want to smile in the face of tragedy.'

Big tits – and a philosopher!

He was just about to launch into his own views on life, death, the troubles and everything, when . . .

'Oh, tea's arrived! Must go. Bye!'

Click.

It didn't matter. Plenty of chances from now on. He felt great. He felt young. He felt the shivering anticipation of a new conquest; the first stirrings of the thrill of the chase. He was arising from the grave of his marriage to a new life, a better life, a sexier life. He didn't fool himself that Joan was other than pure knee-trembling lust; she wasn't in the same emotional league as Warm, Witty, Intelligent, Mature, Professional Lady (P). She was certainly gorgeous-looking, but – he suspected – lightweight, and not given much to art, politics, literature and good conversation. But she would more than fill the gap until Miss Right came along. Yes, things were on the up and up. He'd got his new-build site starting next week. There wasn't a cloud in his sky – that is, if he ignored the gloomy talk of the others across the room. But then, lurking at the back, there was Mary and the separation. And behind that again his next doctor's appointment.

'Hey, lonely pint! Coming to join us?'

He looked up. Pam, a gofer from Steve's department, had joined the group around Tony's desk. She was on a one-year contract and didn't give a curse about anything. Attractive in a tomboyish way, she wasn't really his cup of tea, though he had an inkling that he was hers. Not that she'd actually said anything, but there was something in the way she looked at him. Nice, but a bit wild. Any chance she got she escaped from Steve's attempt at a strict regime. She reckoned the architects were more fun. She was a prized source of information about her boss's plans and eager to share. She was a loose cannon in what Steve considered his tight ship.

She beckoned him over. But Paul's mind was still filled with the long-haired, long-legged images of Joan. Pam would bring him back to reality too soon. He declined.

'Friggin rot there, then!' she said brightly.

Something in the reply reminded him of his wife. He was to call with her that evening.

5

'**O**h, it's you!'

It felt odd knocking on his own front door like a stranger. Mary's greeting confirmed his new status. And yet everything about the place was so familiar: twenty years of living there had made it part of him. Only the FOR SALE sign was new, that and the guarded look in Mary's eyes.

'Well, what is it?'

She didn't invite him in. She stood shielded by the half-opened door as if repelling Jehovah's Witnesses.

He couldn't blame her. He'd been such an arse. Out of the corner of his eye he noticed the hole in the hedge hadn't been fixed – the one she'd pushed him through that last night. But, then, who was to fix it now he wasn't here? Not that there was any guarantee it would have been fixed even if he had been – gardening wasn't his strong point. But the possibility at least was there. And anyway, she was handier at these things. She'd probably left it like that out of spite.

Yes, he'd been a bollox that night. Invited half the rugby club home from the pub – seemed a good idea at the time. She wasn't pleased. The sight of men peeing in her front garden didn't improve her temper and the sound of someone throwing up in the hall was the clincher. Fair enough. She came down in her nightdress and told them all politely to fuck off, which they willingly did, sensing the brewing storm. He was indignant: his friends insulted; he himself humiliated. He ran out of the house after them, arms extended, begging them to come back, never giving up till the last tail lights disappeared round the bend in the road. Outraged, he tussled with Mary, but she fought dirty, punched him in the balls and pushed him into the hedge. Then he slipped on the wet grass and lay on his back in the belting rain with his arms outstretched, wimpering. By this stage Mary had gone back to bed. Only Sambo the cat, ambling delicately with sodden paws over his prone form, remained to observe this final ignominy. He spent that night in the car. Next day he went looking for a flat and the house was put on the market.

'I've come for Sambo.'

She looked blankly at him as if he'd just spoken in a foreign language.

'What?'

Well, right, so there were more pressing issues between two people sundering a twenty-year marriage, but a start had to be made somewhere. And anyway the cat was special: Sambo was his ally. They'd a lot in common, the cat and he. Both had been bad-mouthed by their neighbours. Sambo was accused of begetting numerous other little Sambos about the place; Paul's morals were similarly speculated. upon. They were rogue males in a world of suburban conformity. Both stayed out late, caroused with disreputable characters, climbed fences on occasion, peed in public and slipped into the house quietly together in the small hours – Sambo a black shadow emerging noiselessly from the shrubbery at the sound of Paul's key struggling in the lock.

'You're out teaching all day. I can nip home from the site to feed him like I always did. Makes sense.'

There was another reason. He'd read somewhere that

stroking a cat can lower blood pressure, so Sambo, instead of being merely a flea-bitten pissing machine, could be converted into an unlikely asset. He'd have to change his not very politically correct name, though. Where he now lived, up by the university, was full of prickly students and lefty academics who gave their cats names like Che and Nelson and Fidel.

'The cat's been taken care of,' she announced.

He went cold.

'What!'

He stared at her.

Then Sambo appeared, oozing from between her legs and twining around his own. He breathed again. Then he scooped up the unwilling bundle of fur and nuzzled it.

Just then a man's voice called from the hallway behind. She didn't turn round.

Paul looked at her.

The voice again.

She half turned in acknowledgement, but she held his gaze.

'Jim's going to feed him during the day,' she said.

Jim? Jim? Who the fuck was Jim? Then he put a face to the voice. Ah, no! Ah, frig, no! Jim Ryan! Mr Bigmouth!

'He heard about our . . . situation . . . and he's kindly offered to help.'

Jim what-did-you-have-for-breakfast Ryan! In his house! Feeding his cat! He felt violated.

She at least had the grace to blush. She knew how he hated Ryan. The man was a joke, and when he wasn't a joke he was a troublemaking gossip. Now the hated face joined Mary's at the door opening. She opened it wider.

'Jim's just popped in to see where the feeding trays are.' It was obvious she was embarrassed, uncomfortable.

Ryan wasn't. 'Paul, old son! Settling in OK, are you? I'm,

ah, just giving Mary a hand with her bits and pieces, y'know.'

How could she have taken up with this arsehole! Ryan's own wife left him because he bored her to death. She ran off with a mortuary attendant for a more exciting life.

'Jim's just going now,' said Mary. She looked meaningfully at Ryan.

'Oh, yes. Just going!'

'No. I'm going,' said Paul. He put out a restraining hand. A dignified retreat was called for here.

As he made his way down the drive he heard them talking. He glanced back.

They stood side by side in the doorway. A couple. He was startled to feel a sharp pang of something like jealousy.

Ryan waved. 'Don't worry, Paul . . . I'll take good care of your pussy!'

6

For a few moments the doctor studied him in silence, as if carefully arranging the words suitable for a delicate exchange between doctor and patient.

'You're an insurance man's nightmare, Mr Fox . . .'

Paul waited for the smile. There was none.

'A walking time bomb.'

Paul swallowed.

The doctor looked from Paul to his notes and back again. 'Cholesterol 9.1 . . . Mmmm. Blood pressure 195 over 95!'

He shook his head in the disinterested manner of a punter reading that someone else's horse has just lost.

'We'll have to get you on to treatment right away.' He looked sideways. 'You still sexually active?'

It was the 'still' that annoyed Paul most. Why the question was put was secondary.

'Well . . . yes,' he said.

Sort of. If masturbation counted. And the odd sordid fling after the rugby club on Friday nights. There was Mary of course. But he couldn't even remember the last annual encounter.

'Problem is . . . I'll have to try you on diuretics to start. Know what they are?'

Paul looked blankly at him. He was only half hearing

what was said. He was still taking in the fact that he was a walking time bomb and an insurance man's nightmare. It's not every day you get a lift like that.

'They can interfere with your erectile function.'

Suddenly he had Paul's full attention.

'Pardon?'

'Nasty little buggers.'

'My . . .'

The doctor smiled. 'They can make you impotent.'

'Wha . . .'

''Fraid so. You see . . . Where are you going? Mr Fox . . . I haven't finished my . . .'

Two weeks later he was downing his tenth pint when he remembered that visit. He was instantly sober. Up till then he'd managed to put it out of his mind. But present prospects brought it to the fore.

'C'mon, Paul, love! Taxi's here!'

Claire leaned over him, her heavily scented breasts on offer within inches of his face.

It was Friday night in the rugby club members-only bar, a night sacred to chasing men and unattached women. Wives knew to give it a wide berth – it was the boys' night out. Claire was almost one of the boys. She was a divorcée who liked to mix in with the lads. She was a great thrower of spontaneous after-club parties and she had grappled with most of the members in her time, and with other body parts as well if she particularly liked someone. Tonight was shaping up to be Paul's turn.

But suddenly he wasn't fussed. The thought of the doctor depressed him. He'd have to go on those tablets, of course he would. It was stupid running out like that. But – impotence! The very word seemed to have a draining effect. Was this to be the title of the last chapter in his someday autobiography:

'The Viagra Years'? Was this to be the end of his fruitful maledom? His biological clock suspended for ever at half past six. Cock death.

In the taxi Claire was all over him. A sudden panic – what if even thinking about it brought it on? He thought he should check his equipment. But Claire did it for him.

He passed.

7

His new site had been running for about eight weeks when he first noticed the man on crutches standing at the entrance gate. He stood there doing nothing, just looking in. As Paul's car swept past, a spray of mud and stones engulfed him. He didn't move. Paul turned to mouth an apology. The man took no notice, just kept staring into the site. Not the full shilling. A lot of that about. A vast home for the bewildered, some of these estates. 'Inbreeding,' Danny, the clerk of works, said. Rumour had it that some family trees hereabouts didn't fork. 'Through each other like rabbits,' he said.

Then he recognised the man: one of the brickies. Hadn't seen him about the site lately. Not – now he came to think of it – since the time of the leg-breaking episode.

He wondered.

Just inside the entrance two upended wellington boots poked skyward from a mound of clay. A note dangled from one: HERE LIES DANNY. RIP.

The brickies.

Deadly enemies, the brickies and Danny. Their life's work was to get away with as little as possible; his job as clerk of works was to stop them. Deadly enemies, but yet between them there was the sneaking regard of one cute hoor for another. They were a match in all but numbers. But being outnumbered was no worry to Danny. Alert as a hen, a lifetime of dealing with slippery customers had rendered him almost mute. His silences did his talking for him. 'Whatever y'say, say nothin.' No hostages to fortune for him. He never signed anything; was never known to say yes; was big on inference and innuendo; spoke between his own lines. 'Say nothin till y'hear more' was his mantra. He would never use two words if one would do; would never use a word if a nod or a wink or a nudge would do – and while this visual semaphore was fine in a face-to-face situation, it wasn't so handy over the phone. This reticence disciplined his features. They rarely registered emotion. Only the darting eyes hinted at the high-octane material behind. The mouth a straight line, even when talking. 'Sure that hoor cud whisper in his own ear,' was the brickies' reluctant tribute.

Today Paul's site visit was, in a manner of speaking, on doctor's orders. It was to be a form of cardiovascular therapy. And he was going to enjoy it. He was about to dump on the builder from a great height – something he'd wanted to do for a long time but never had, and ended up hating himself for it. Now, for his health's sake, he would do what he thought was right. It had to be faced: much of the brickwork was rubbish; he would have it knocked down and rebuilt. Simple as that. End of story. Of course, the builder wouldn't be happy. Frig' em! From now on he was looking after number one! He was a different person now. He wasn't bottling things up any more. No, no more of that. No more buried resentment. No more Mr Nice Guy. Wanting to be Mr Nice Guy took its toll. It raised his blood pressure. It was zero tolerance from now on. And today he had a good moral launching pad for his crusade: Danny had found a mislaid cheese sandwich freshly mortared into a joint in a brick wall. That part of the wall would have to be rebuilt. A house built upon a cheese sandwich cannot stand; that would be his text for today.

The builder and Maguire, his surveyor, awaited him in the hut. First time he'd met them was at the start-up meeting back in the office. At such a meeting the architect would be confronted with a tieless countryman with straw in his hair, hands like shovels, who could barely write his name but had an extramural doctorate in cute hoorism. This was the builder. Beside him would be a smoothie in a five-hundred-pound suit, smoking an expensive cigar; this would be the surveyor. He would have a similar qualification but with a smattering of quantity surveying and elocution thrown in. Such a man was Maguire; and such a builder was Leo P. Runian, constructional engineer.

'And how are you, Paul, old son?'

Maguire, oozing bonhomie, was a walking cliché of insincerity. With his full, red and fleshy face, he gave the air of someone perpetually well wined and dined. Paul wondered what his blood pressure was – could probably drive a steam engine. He seemed out of place in the hut. The whiff of deodorant, his year-round tan, his jet-black fifty-year-old hair, his expensive well-fitting suit, the golden blaze of watch, ring and bracelet beneath the immaculate cuffs – all this set him apart from the wellington-booted shabbiness around him. He gave the impression of a man used to better things, a man completely on top of events.

Paul was now about to knock him off.

'There . . . a few repair items to be getting on with!'

He was savouring the anticipated reaction as he presented the builder with a list of the work he reckoned wasn't up to standard and would have to be redone. The items covered two full A4 sheets.

They stared at the list. Then at him.

Runian brought his face close. He smiled uneasily.

'A joke, right?'

Paul shook his head.

Maguire looked like he'd just had a bereavement.

'You can't be serious! Cost us a bloody fortune, that will!' he said. 'We're talking telephone numbers here!'

'Conlig 4?'

Nobody laughed at Paul's quip. Not even Danny. No lover of builders, he – but he hated to see a dumb animal suffer. He looked at Paul. They all did.

This wasn't the compliant Paul they were used to and expected. He knew everybody saw him as someone who avoided unpleasantness, who didn't get mad; someone easy to deal with, who played the game. In other words: a pushover.

But no more. No more Mr Nice Guy. Mr Nice Guys died young. Mr Evil Bastard from now on. Henceforth he would measure his health by his unpopularity. Happy builder bad; sad builder good.

Later he saw the news spread through the site as the foreman moved among the squads of men, telling them what would have to be redone – and at their own expense. The brickies straightened up from their work, tipping back the peaks of their baseball caps with their trowels, and stared across at Paul.

He was the most hated man on the site. It felt great.

It was only when he got home that he found scratched down the side of his car YOUR PUTTIN OUT OUR LITE.

8

It was ages before Paul heard from Joan again. Housing management inhabited a different floor and a different world. Normally the architects hated to hear from housing officers. It meant problems with repairs, complaining tenants, trouble. Their job, then, was to get the builders back – something the builders were always reluctant to do, as there was no money in it for them.

But with Joan it was different. He was happy to hear from her any time.

'I'm only here a sec, Paul. I was up seeing Brian – Mr Johnson – about a matter and I thought I'd kill two birds with one stone.'

Johnson was a senior architect to whom the various architectural teams – Ken's among them – reported. He in turn reported to a regional architect, who reported to the directors, who reported to the council manager. Although he was fairly well down the chain of command, Johnson nevertheless wielded great influence in the area of the city that he serviced. However, he was a man whom Paul rarely encountered, preferring, as he did, to deal solely with people of team leader level and above. Joan's easy familiarity with him – bypassing Ken, Paul and the other lesser lights – was an indicator of the reduced status of the technical people in an increasingly management-oriented organisation.

She was flushed and breathless from the stairs. She looked magnificent.

'Pa-ul . . .'

His name slowly unfurled itself from her lips like a caress.

'. . . we've got a difficult tenant . . . customer . . . threatening to write about us to the papers, the TV, to the prime minister, the queen, the United Nations, everybody. Anyway, it would be bad publicity. You know the sort of thing.'

He nodded abstractly. Wonderful breasts.

'It's your rehab site, the one you've just finished . . .'

He hauled his eyes upwards. 'Prince Charles Mews?'

''Fraid so.'

Paul groaned.

'Seems his toilet's blocked and he says he can't get the builder back to fix it. The man sounds quite mad actually.'

'He'll not be alone down there, then.'

'You're awful, Paul!' She laughed and gave his shoulder a playful flick. He felt his knees tremble. 'Anyway, I tried to explain the procedure to him. He had to inform us first and we'd get the architect to instruct the builder to action it. But he just rants away about the builder . . .' She dropped her eyes. 'He's a bit sectarian actually about the builder . . .'

Talking about religion was distasteful, especially when you didn't know who was who.

'Anyway, Brian – Mr Johnson – asked me to go down and talk to him, y'know, do a PR job. Might calm him down . . .' Then she looked straight at him, her deep blue eyes appealing. 'I was wondering, Paul . . . It would be a great support, from a technical point of view, if you could come with me.'

Normally Paul would rather have an operation for piles with a rusty razor blade than face an awkward tenant. But not now. This was a dream coming true.

'Ah, thanks a million, Paul!' She reached out and gripped him in brothers-in-arms solidarity. He didn't feel brotherly.

She was just about to let go of him when he felt an unmerciful blatter on the back of the head and sheets of paper cascaded around his shoulders.

He swung round as Pam flounced off across the room. She shouted over her shoulder.

'Your job reports.' Then, giving Joan a glare, 'If you've time to read them!'

What was that about!

'Bloody hell!'

But secretly he was pleased. There could be only one explanation. Even though he'd never as much as looked at her, the poor thing was jealous!

He smiled. He still had what it takes.

9

The clubhouse stretched along one side of the playing pitch. The bar on the first floor was all window on one wall, giving an uninterrupted view of the action below. Here the alicadoos would gather every Saturday to watch the game and mix with friends. They would share memories of their sporting youth, praising each other's past exploits, comparing the teams of today with their own time, all delighting in each other's company, regarding each other with the uncritical love that only one ex-rugby player can feel for another. And from this would spring a quite natural freemasonry of business contacts. After all, the man with whom you shared the spills and dangers of the sports field would be the man you happily did business with. So it was with Roy, a rep for a brick, cement and concrete company. Where possible, Paul would specify his bricks, thus cementing in a suitably concrete form an acquaintance of almost twenty years. Roy for his part would see to it that Paul's contracts got priority service – though lately Paul had begun to have the unworthy suspicion that the bricks he was getting weren't first quality. But he had kept this to himself. Yes, the clubhouse served many needs – and to add to its attractions, it was generally a woman-free zone.

'See you, Paul –' Roy pushed his sweaty face up close –

'you're one evil hoor!'

There was no higher praise.

'Will y'ever forget that Ballymena game in the Cup ... June 90?' His eyes bored into Paul's. 'Time you grabbed that big fella's balls in the lineout? One bad hoor you were.' His eyes twinkled.

Paul smiled modestly. He hadn't meant it. Pure accident as his hand reached out to steady himself. But the myth had grown. His reputation rose with it.

'Then he turns and punches me! Me! God, that was a good'un!' Roy laughed and thumped the table. 'A bloody good'un, ay! What an eejit!'

Memories of Roy's black and blue face laughing at the thought of the Ballymena player hitting the wrong man. Hilarious – only to Roy. He was still laughing when they carted him off to have a brain scan.

It was then Paul first thought of getting out, getting out when he still had his teeth, normal-sized ears, a straight nose and his marbles. Roy was a warning of what too many knocks on the head can do to you. Mary had been at him to give up. She said he was making a fool of himself, togging out with eighteen-year-olds when he was pushing forty. People would think he was some sort of pervert. His attitude was that if he was good enough to keep his place, why shouldn't he? She said when was he ever going to grow up?

That was the difference between them: to her growing up meant not having fun any more. It meant coffee mornings with boring people; playing bridge; visiting people you didn't like and – worse – having them visit you. It meant not getting drunk with your mates; no more chasing; no more everything that made life worth living. It meant going everywhere in couples. It meant stagnation. Well, fuck all that! He wasn't ready for that. Never would be. All that was for oldies. He'd see some of them in the club, old alicadoos fettered to their wives: once great roaring men – now neutered toms, with their spouses counting their drinks. Not a pretty sight.

Anyway, he didn't consider himself a proper alicadoo. Alicadoos were old men – he'd only stopped playing five years ago, for God's sake. He'd carried on far longer than most of his former team mates. And he was proud of it; proud of himself, proud of his physique. He looked around at the others. A sorry sight. Let themselves go, most of them. Lots of grey hair. Some dyed, mostly badly; a few tastefully like his own. A few completely bald. Two wigs. Numerous bent noses. One new hip. A fair crop of false teeth and cauliflower ears. A couple of dodgy prostates. At least one missing testicle. A rumoured artificial penis. And lots of beer bellies. No excuse for those; he saw to it that exercise preserved his washboard stomach. Mary often said he'd a better figure than she had. And – though he said it himself – he had. But she always said it with a bit of a smirk. Why shouldn't he be proud of his shape? They say men over fifty aren't noticed by women. Well, he bloody well wasn't going to be one.

'Paul . . .'

Roy suddenly grabbed his arm. His stare was even more intense than before, but the joy had left his eyes.

Roy was completely bald. He'd been expounding his theory about baldness: he'd noted how many bald ex-rugby players there were and he put it down to all that hairwashing after matches and practice. Hygiene was the enemy of hair, he reckoned.

'Did you ever see a bald tramp?'

Paul had been considering this weighty matter when Roy was overcome by a mood change.

'Paul –' his grip tightened – 'me oul mate . . .'

Paul flinched at the serious tone. They were at the eight-pint stage. A bit late for serious.

'Sorry to hear about ... y'know ...'

His chubby beer-flecked finger toyed with a beer mat.

Oh no. Paul squirmed. He guessed what was coming.

'You and Mary...'

This was uncharted territory.

'Bad job,' said Roy. 'Bad bloody job!'

He dropped his voice. He looked around. Not suitable for bar conversation, that sort of talk. Indecent almost. Men didn't talk about such things, close things. For them, jokes and loud laughs leavened most conversations. Mostly they were the conversations. They could and did talk about sex, murder, politics, sport, everything. But relationships – never. And while four-letter words were the order of the day, there was one that was rarely heard: love.

Paul nodded his appreciation.

Roy shook his head sadly.

But Paul's situation wasn't that unusual. Looking around his friends, he reckoned about a third were divorced or separated. Others were in second and third marriages. There were a few bachelors – one of questionable sexual orientation who was always sure of space in the showers. From what he could tell, most of the marriages seemed to vary from so-so to unhappy. Only one person admitted to being happily married, but he'd never anything interesting to say. Nobody bothered with him.

He loved this place. The people. The air of excitement on match day. The team photos on the wall, himself among them, charting his decline from a youthful black-haired Adonis, when he played for the Firsts, to the greying mature man in the Fourths.

Yes, a huge slice of his life was here. Here he was safe and secure, with the tang of his own kind around him. The worlds of home and work were far away. He shut them out for this time to himself. His problems existed in another realm. They could wait.

10

'Impotence isn't guaranteed.'

The doctor made it sound like a lottery prize.

'It's a risk, a side effect for some people. Just some.'

Shame-faced, he'd crept back to confront whatever had to be confronted. The doctor said he should count himself lucky how little was wrong with him. He was entering that stage of life in men when things begin to stop working, clog up, drop down or drop off.

'I've just sent a patient for prostate investigation,' he said. 'It means having a camera pushed up his penis. How would you like that, then?'

Paul was still dwelling on the dimensions of his Olympus when the doctor produced the tablets.

'And there's all you have to complain about.' He jiggled the blister pack in his hand.

They looked harmless enough. But already he felt his scrotum tightening in anticipation. He had prided himself on never having taken a pill in his life. His body was a temple to nature's remedies. No alien chemical had knowingly entered his bloodstream. Now he read from the packet what he would be ingesting: Lercanidipine, lactose monohydrate, microcrystalline, polyvinylpyrrolidone, methylhydroxpropylcellulose, macrogol, ferric oxide, etc. Each word enough to choke a donkey. Then listed on the back were the possible side effects: loss of appetite, stomach upsets, dehydration, impotence, increased blood cholesterol, allergic reactions, increased uric acid (leading to risk of gout), rise in blood sugar.

Jesus!

He panicked.

'Do I have to take them?'

He felt every side effect in anticipation. He'd become a one-man pandemic merely by holding the packet!

'Frankly, Mr Fox, you've no choice. We just have to get that blood pressure under control. You run a greatly increased risk of stroke, heart attack, angina, kidney damage, sight problems.' He paused, then smiled. 'Anyway, let's face it, if its impotence you're worried about, there's much more to life than sex, isn't there?'

Paul looked at the doctor's skinny frame, his bad teeth, his thinning hair. For you, maybe, he thought. He smirked, but said nothing.

'At our time of life, who could be bothered with small children running about the place, ay?'

Who was talking about children? Sex was the subject. And anyway, what's this 'our time'! He didn't want to be bracketed with this skinny weed. They might be of an age, but that was all.

'How many children have you, Mr Fox?'

Paul ignored the question.

But he persisted. 'How many?'

The question always made him uncomfortable. As did the invariable response to his reply.

'None.'

'Oh.'

There it was again: the sympathising tone. The more he looked at the doctor, the more convinced he was he'd never had a woman. Something about him. Probably gay. What would a woman see in him? Who would want a little pip-squeak like that on top of her anyway? He almost felt sorry for him. But still he couldn't resist a bit of a dig.

His eyes narrowed knowingly.

'Y'know, there's more to sex than babies, doctor.'

The doctor swept him towards the door. His time was at an end.

'I'm glad to hear that,' he said. 'I've got seven!'

He had a bad night that night, thinking about the imminent demise of his sex life. And when he got into the office next morning nothing but gloom awaited him there as well. The organisation's new market-testing computer system was beginning to spew out results and they weren't welcome. The news that most of their jobs were making losses sent the architects into a downer. Paul was already depressed. He had taken his first pill that morning and was experiencing every one of the listed side effects – except insomnia. He was saving that for bedtime.

Tony, however, was upbeat. 'How can you measure service to the public?' he announced. 'Those results are meaningless. Ignore them.'

The others rumbled in agreement. But the unease was there.

11

Life in the flat was cramped, cold and lonely. He missed Sambo. And, surprisingly, he missed Mary, if only as somebody to have around. He supposed she hardly missed him with that arsehole Ryan worming his way in. He missed the jobs she did. There was something wrong with the light switch; she would have mended it in minutes. He knew nothing about electricity. Also he was useless at cooking. Consequently he was eating out a lot and spending time in the club and drinking more than he should. All costing a fortune. The sooner the house was sold, the sooner he'd be able to buy a place of his own. And yet – he was uneasy about it, this final cutting of the link. But Mary insisted. So each time he heard her voice on the phone updating him on the sale, his stomach tightened.

'Paul . . .'

His reaction this time was no different.

But her message was: 'Some fucker's just thrown a brick through the window!'

Her Swiss finishing school always surfaced in times of stress.

'What!'

'A whole brick! I could've been killed! Will I ring the police? . . . What'll I do, Paul?'

This wasn't like her; she always knew what to do. She was definitely spooked.

He was over in ten minutes.

Two large policemen filled the living room. Drinking tea. Their feet and legs were everywhere. One fat one standing, the other seated and balancing a notebook on his knee. They were jollying her along, but they became serious when he entered.

'Evening, sir!' said the fat one.

At the same moment Bigmouth entered from the kitchen with a dustpan and began helping Mary pick up the shards of glass.

'Right mess, Paul,' he said.

The writing policeman looked up and fixed Paul with a penetrating stare.

'You live around here, sir?'

'No. I . . .'

At that Mary came in with more tea.

'Oh, that's Paul –' She hesitated. 'My husband.'

The policeman looked at Bigmouth. 'Oh, sorry. I thought . . .'

'We're separated,' she explained.

The two policemen exchanged a knowing look.

'I see,' said the fat one, standing with his thumbs tucked into his flack jacket. 'So you live elsewhere, then, sir?'

Paul could see his brain working. Hercule Poirot was on the case.

'If you don't mind me asking, sir, where were you about thirty minutes ago?'

'Me!'

'Oh, no, constable, you don't think . . .' said Mary.

'I'm only asking a question.'

'But he's my husband! You can't believe . . .'

'When you've seen as many domestics as I have, you

believe anything. Well, sir?'

Bigmouth and the two policemen stared at him. Christ's sake, they thought he bloody did it!

Sambo was picking his way towards him through the fragments of glass. He scooped him up, showing the policemen that somebody who was this nice with animals wouldn't throw bricks through anybody's window. For extra measure he scratched his belly and under his chin. Sambo responded by rolling on his back and stretching out his front and back legs full-length – his party trick. Paul cradled him like a baby, smiling at the policemen for their approval.

They weren't impressed.

'Well, sir?'

He felt he was on trial.

'You serious?'

The fat one glowered seriously.

He gave chapter and verse of his movements.

'Can anyone corroborate this, sir?' said the fat one.

The thin one just sat quietly taking notes.

Paul felt the engine rods going. Normally he was quite timid before the majesty of the law. No longer.

'Now hold on here! It's a broken friggin window, not mass murder!'

Bad move. He saw the darkening brow. But the seated one, who appeared to be higher up the food chain and had some gumption, stood up and led the other out of the house, saying they had got enough to go on with for the moment.

'Probably kids anyway,' said Paul.

'Yes, that's all, Mary. Kids. Don't you worry,' comforted Bigmouth.

'They weren't kids,' said Mary. 'I heard them shouting.'

'What'd they say?' said Paul.

'Didn't make sense.'

'What was it?'

'Something like ... "You put out our light ... we'll put out yours." What's that supposed to mean?'

'Haven't a clue,' said Bigmouth. 'You any idea, Paul?'

He was on the phone to Danny first thing.

'Did I ever leave my address there? On an envelope or anything?'

'No.'

'In the hut? Anywhere the brickies might find it?'

'No. Why would you?'

'Precisely.'

'What?'

'I never would. Then how come those bastards know where I live?'

Or more accurately, where he used to live, but that was none of Danny's business.

There was a silence for a bit.

'Oh.' Danny's voice was subdued.

'What?'

'Something happen?'

'A brick through the window, that's what happened!'

'Oh.'

'Them all right. I'm sure of it.'

Danny sighed. 'Likely!'

'What?'

'Same every time.'

'Y'mean it's happened before?'

'Oh, aye.'

'Who to?'

'Anyone annoys them.'

'But my address ... how?'

'Not here.' Danny was defensive.

'But where?'

'Where are your records kept?'

'Wha? Here in the council offices, of course. Personnel department. Sure, where else would they be kept!'

'Well ...'

'Well what?'

'That's where they've been got.'

'Y'mean ... But how?'

'Ways.'

'Y'mean somebody in here ...'

'Possibly.'

'But who? Why?'

'Must go.'

Click.

12

Singledom was great – except for the being on your own bit. He and Mary hadn't much going for them, but at least she was life about the place. He missed the sounds of her: the whirring of drills, the rasping of saws. He missed even the aggrieved scowls she gave as he fled the house in the mornings; the snarled greeting as he returned home at night. No, man wasn't meant to live alone. He needed companionship, anybody's companionship. He wanted affection. He wanted respect. And he knew the only sure place where all these were to be found.

Sambo.

A number of times he'd reached for the phone, about to ring her. But he stopped. She'd never believe it was the cat he was after. She was waiting for him to crack. Well, she could wait. He wouldn't be the one to crawl back. And anyway, why would he when he had a whole new world before him – a single world, a world of endless possibilities. It was all out there, waiting for him. A fresh start. A new leaf. A new love.

He was in this hopeful frame of mind when, rummaging for change, he dredged up a familiar-looking piece of newspaper. He straightened out the creases with his thumb and forefinger.

JANE: WARM, WITTY, INTELLIGENT, MATURE, PROFESSIONAL LADY (P) . . .

God, he'd almost forgotten.

Suddenly he was tempted.

And why not? He needed companionship, no doubt about that. And sex. OK, he mightn't have been much of a husband, but he wasn't cut out for bachelorhood; he needed someone to live with. Cooped up in his flat, he was starting to get cabin fever. No, he definitely wasn't made to be a loner. Loners were oddballs, misfits, religious maniacs, child molesters and serial killers. He needed a companion or a wife. Or at least a woman.

Should he ring? But what to say? Would he sound an awful eejit? Would she hear in his voice this pathetic lonely creature crying out for love? Begging for it? Probably. But then, that's what she herself was doing, wasn't it?

To hell! Faint heart ne'er won fair lady! But still he hesitated. He remembered all the jokes about Lonely Hearts dating. Only life's failures did that, he reckoned. And perverts. What did that make him now!

His finger shook as he tapped the numbers. His trembling surprised him. But then, it was only natural. After all, it's not a thing you'd do every day, this.

His breathing roared back at him from the mouthpiece. He tried to control it. She might mistake him for . . .

'Hello?'

The voice was low, sensuous. Yet wary. World full of psychos; a woman couldn't be too careful. He would tread delicately here. First impressions were so important. He composed himself carefully, making sure he was seated comfortably, controlling his breathing, pursing his lips ready to launch into his introductory spiel –

Brrrrrrrrrr . . .

The phone rang off. He'd delayed too long. Friggin frightened her off!

Bugger!

He rang back quickly. Nerves jangling.

As the phone was lifted he rushed to be first to speak. He couldn't afford to make a bollox of it a second time.

'Look, I'm awfully sorry. Really stupid, that. That was me ringing there now. I hope you didn't think I was some pervert. Bad way to start getting to know someone. It was just that . . .' He was suddenly conscious of the silence at the other end. 'Hello?'

'Wrong number, mate!' gruffed a male voice.

Brrrrrrrr.

Jesus!

Third time lucky.

'Hello?'

Low, sensuous. But even more cautious.

'Sorry. Look . . . my apologies . . . that was me ringing a few minutes ago . . .'

Silence.

'It's about your ad in the paper . . .'

'Oh?'

Success! A first hint of welcome.

'Jane, isn't it?'

'Yes.'

Sounded very nice.

'Look, I've never done this sort of thing before . . .'

'God, nor have I.' She giggled.

He felt more confident.

'Look . . . I was wondering . . . could we meet for a drink or something . . . or whatever people do?'

'Well . . .'

'Or whatever . . . anything . . . anywhere . . . y'know . . .'

'A drink would be fine, sure. A drink, yes . . . great.'

He could feel her warm to him. It was his low voice. People said he had a sexy voice. He dropped it a bit more.

'Suppose you should know something about me. Well, for starters I'm forty-one ... six foot tall ... thirteen and a half stone ... dark hair ... divorced ... no children.' She'd never notice the few years he'd knocked off. 'And what about ...'

'Me? OK ... Well, I'm thirty-nine ... also divorced ... but with two little girls, eight and six.' Pause. An anxious note: 'Is that a problem?'

'No.' Well, not at this stage.

'I'm blonde, five seven,' she continued. Then laughed. 'I'm told I'm quite good-looking. I've got a good figure. Perhaps a little more curvaceous than average – but, then, I believe that's what you men like, isn't it?'

He was instantly aroused. She was selling herself to him.

'Oh, yes, I like that very much.' He gave a throaty laugh. He felt a warm glow. Hey, this could be nice. But he needed some background. 'What do you do?'

'Do?'

'For a living ... Do you work?'

'Oh, yes, I work. Have to.'

'What at?'

'I'm an architect.'

'What!'

'An architect.'

'I don't believe you!'

'Pardon?'

'You're joking ... an architect!' He laughed. 'Ah ... Holy God!'

'And what's funny about that?' She mistook his laugh. Suddenly there was ice in her voice. For a brief moment it sounded familiar.

'Oh, nothing ... nothing. It's just ... see ... I'm an architect too!'

'You serious? Goodness!' She relaxed into warmth again.

'Hey, there's a great start, isn't it? . . . Oh, by the way, my name's Paul.'

She laughed. 'Hi, Paul.' Then, dropping her voice, 'You sound really nice.'

Again the warmth flooding his loins. 'So do you, Jane.'

'Y'know something . . . I think I'm really looking forward to seeing you, Paul.'

'Same here, Jane.' He was definitely getting the vibes.

Then a thought, a faintly disturbing thought. Both architects in a smallish city. Surely their paths must have crossed. But, anyway, he didn't know any Jane architects.

'By the way . . . Jane isn't my real name.'

'Oh . . .'

'No. I just used it for the advert . . . You can't be too careful.'

A faint chill ran up his spine.

'Y'know . . . your voice really does sound terribly familiar.' Something niggled at the back of his mind. Where had he heard it?

'So does yours, Paul. It's almost as if –' she hesitated – 'as if we already know each other.' She giggled.

He giggled to, but his unease was growing.

'So . . . well . . . what is it?'

'What?'

'Your real name . . .'

'Oh . . . ' He sensed her hesitancy. 'It's . . . Stella.'

He could tell she heard the sharp intake of his breath.

'Paul?'

He couldn't speak.

'Something wrong?'

He wanted to run.

'Do you . . . think you know me? 'Apprehension in her voice. 'Don't think I know any Paul architects . . . That is . . .'

Then her own intake of breath. 'Oh, no ... Oh, shit! Is that ... ?'

He slammed the phone down.

Fuuuuuuuuuuuuuuuck!

Joan picked him up at the front door of the building. He was showered, shaved and had his new aftershave on. He was shaking. He felt as if he was on his first date. It didn't help that all morning he and Stella had been trying to avoid eye contact. By mutual unspoken consent, that phone call had never happened. It was a secret to be taken to the grave.

'Cold out,' he said, clambering in.

'Think so?'

She obviously didn't. Her knees and lower thighs protruded from her miniskirt like two brown boiled eggs. He tried to keep his eyes off them as her feet worked the pedals. He noted his pills weren't going to be a problem.

'Thanks for coming, Paul. Useful to have somebody technical on hand, in case ... y'know ... he asks anything ... well ... technical.' She turned her big eyes on him again. 'Don't mind, do you?'

'No problem.'

And it wasn't – at the start, anyway, as he tried to impress her with his sparkling wit. It was only as they reached the estate with the red, white and blue painted kerbstones and the large brick wall bearing the words ONE FAITH, ONE CROWN. NO POPE IN OUR TOWN that it occurred to him he'd never asked her the exact address. As she turned into the familiar cul-de-sac he started to have a bad feeling. As she pulled up outside the house with the plastic number 7 dangling unluckily from a nail, he knew what it was.

'You OK, Paul?'

'Fine.'

'You've gone a funny colour.'

'It's just . . . really depressing, these places.'

They were walking up the path. He hadn't told her about his previous visit; made him sound like a wimp. He was taking a gamble that the man would be out. If he was, fine. He'd make excuses to get out of any future visit, having shown willing once. If he was in, he'd just bluff it out. He'd say he forgot. He hoped against hope he was out.

She knocked on the door.

''S fuckin open!'

Sunk.

As before, the invitation came from far inside. They went in.

He whispered in the hall. 'Oh . . . I remember now. I've been . . .'

'Grrrr.'

The dog appeared in front of them. He'd forgotten about it.

'Grrrrr. Grrrrr.'

Paul manoeuvred himself behind Joan.

'Yer a'right! Only wants to nose you!' called the familiar voice from the living room.

Paul froze.

The dog looked at him with no flicker of recognition. It had a dilemma, which it quickly resolved. Faced with a choice of crotches, it launched its nose into Joan's. Good taste, Paul acknowledged. He was wondering what he could do to save her when she knelt down and pulled the dog's face against her own.

'Who's a lovely girl, then?' she said, ruffling the animal's ears! She smiled up at Paul. 'Friendly, isn't she? Here, give her a stroke.'

He forced a smile.

'Go on!'

He chanced a rigid hand.

'Grrrr.'

The dog wasn't fooled.

The hand was quickly withdrawn.

The man now appeared in the hall. He was barefoot, but wearing jeans and an egg-stained cream shirt that had once been white. The shirt was unbuttoned down the front and his flies had not been zipped fully; a tuck of shirt poked out. He looked even more naked than at the first encounter.

'Yous from the council?'

'We've come about your problem,' said Joan.

He peered at Paul. He gave a sneer of recognition.

'See you've brought yours with yeh.'

'Hello again.' Paul gave a weak smile.

Joan was brisk. 'May we have a look at the toilet? Where ...'

'Follow yer nose.'

The smell hit them at the bottom of the stairs. As they ascended it got worse. It was a physical presence that had to be leaned into to proceed.

The man went ahead. He threw open the bathroom door and stood to one side, arm extended, as if revealing a prize exhibit. Paul's stomach heaved. The toilet bowl was overflowing with solid matter. Newspapers were spread around the floor and dotted on these were little piles of turds. The smell was overpowering. It filled every orifice like cotton wool. It soaked through every pore.

'Shithouse, init?' he announced with pride and accuracy.

One glance was enough for Joan. She blanched and turned for the stairs.

'Shithouse! Geddit?' He laughed at his own joke.

As he turned to close the door, Joan looked at Paul, cast her eyes up and twiddled her finger at the side of her head.

Downstairs, she tried to take control of the situation. 'You've been using the bathroom as a toilet, Mr Brown?'

'Where do you suggest I shite? The livin friggin room?'

'Look, we'll see that your toilet is unblocked right away.' She turned to Paul.

'Right, Paul? You'll contact the builder?' She turned back to the man. 'But why didn't you complain before?'

'Complain? Complain?' He looked from one to the other. His eyes bulged. 'Wasn't I out every day after the frigger of a plumber. And every day he says he's comin – and that's the last I see of him. All promises like all yous council ones!'

Joan looked at Paul. The man stood directly in front of him.

Paul dropped his head to avoid the mad eyes. 'We'll get the plumber back right away,' he muttered.

'That OK, Mr Brown?' Joan edged towards the door, mission hopefully accomplished.

He glowered at her. 'Too late. Get somebody else!'

She stopped.

'Pardon?'

'Wouldn't have that hoor about me now.'

Joan glanced quickly at Paul. 'But he's the plumber for this job!'

'He's had his chance.'

'But, Mr Brown . . .'

He leaned forward, eyes bulging. 'I'm tellin you now, if that fenian bastard puts a foot over my door, I'll stick his head in that bowl up there!'

Exit time.

Paul looked round for the dog.

Joan was still trying to keep control. 'But if you won't let us fix it . . .'

He snarled. 'You deaf? I'm sayin I want another plumber. A protestant plumber.'

'But, Mr Brown . . .'

'You want me to shite in the livin room?'

'Mr Brown!'

Paul tugged her sleeve, drawing her to the door.

The man saw. 'Here, you! I seen you over on that new site. No shortage of plumbers over there, ay? Get everythin they want! All fenians over there of course.'

In the hall. His hand on the door knob. Joan now as keen to make an escape as he was.

'Well, Mr Brown, we'll see what can be done.'

The man narrowed his eyes. 'Think us ones over here don't know what's goin on, ay?'

Paul was fiddling with the knob. It wouldn't turn. Something slippery on it. He didn't dare speculate.

'Oh, aye, we see all the comins and goins. An' there's boys here don't like what they see: them gettin everythin and us uns left in our shite.'

The knob turned. Joan got through first. Paul jammed in his eagerness to get out. The dog appeared, nosed him briefly and went away. He was out.

'Goodbye, Mr Brown! Remember, we're here to help!'

Joan managed to keep her optimistic customer-is-always-right brightness. Management training paid off in such situations.

'Away an' fuck yerself!' said Mr Brown.

Driving back to the office Joan tried to regain her composure, but the encounter with the highly esteemed customer had taken its toll. She was white. She said she felt sick. Paul took over the driving, was thrilled to do so. For these brief few minutes she was in his hands, was depending on him. It felt good.

'Uuuugh, I need a shower and a change of clothes ... something to get rid of this smell. Uuuuuggh!'

His mind played with images of her in her bathroom. 'Will I drive you home, Joan?'

'No. Just take me back to the office. I'll go up right away and tell Brian ... er ... Mr Johnson exactly what our Mr Brown is like.'

As she got out of the car and headed for the entrance, it occurred to him that she'd forgotten about her shower and change of clothes.

13

Nowadays he was hardly ever in the office. Just couldn't face Stella. The horror in her eyes mirrored his own. He woke at nights with the nightmare of it all. What if the others ever found out? Social crucifixion. The walk past her work station was a Via Dolorosa of embarrassment. Once at going-home time he was in the lift with Tony when she rushed in at the last minute. Seeing Paul, she tried to retreat, but the door was already closing. Paul squeezed himself into a corner. Avoid eye contact at all costs.

'Can't get away quick enough, ay?' joked Tony.

'You're dead right.' She stared straight ahead at the back of the closing doors.

Silence ensued until the doors opened again on the ground floor. Tony and Stella were first out, rushing for the car park

''Night, Stella . . . Paul,' said Tony.

''Night, Tony . . . Paul,' said Stella.

''Night, Tony . . . Jane!'

Aaaaahhhhh!

He could have bitten his tongue off. It just came out.

She turned and withered him with a look.

Tony turned also, looking from one to the other. 'Jane? Who the hell's Jane!'

No, the site nowadays was a much more inviting place.

Nothing disgruntled brickies could inflict on him was a patch on this exquisite suffering. And anyway life was so simple now that everything had to be by the book. Mr Evil Bastard was in charge now. Mr Evil Bastard kept the stresses at bay. If a thing wasn't perfect, it had to be redone. Full stop. No arguments. No agonising over decisions. No compromises. Now every time he left the site the unhappiness of the brickies was the measure of his success, an index of his cardiovascular health. And there were no more broken windows. He reckoned he'd shown them who was boss.

But Danny wasn't so sure. 'Bidin their time, those uns.'

It was Mary on the phone. Sambo had disappeared. Went out last night and hadn't returned.

'Got a lady friend maybe. He's only human,' he tried to console her.

'Like you, y'mean.'

'It's only a joke, Mary!' She was losing her sense of humour. Going odd on her own maybe.

She rarely rang him at the office. And even less so since they split up. But aside from the cat, there was other mutual business to be discussed.

'There's a couple coming to view tonight. Want to be there?' It was her take-it-or-leave-it tone.

Of course he did. It was his home too.

That evening as she opened the door the aroma of freshly baked bread wafted against him. He staggered back. Mary baking bread! The smell of dry rot fluid or tile adhesive or sawn wood would have been more the norm. In the background soft violin music.

'It said in a magazine how to make your house welcoming to prospective buyers,' she explained.

There was no freshly baked bread; she'd merely bought

the smell. There wasn't a glimpse of a power tool, or a saw, or odds and ends of timber lying around. Instead everywhere was swept and tidy, with strategically placed vases of flowers. A fire crackled in the grate.

'Why can't it be like this all the time?' he said.

She pulled a face.

She even looked different herself. Gone were the dusty tracksuit bottoms and stained T-shirt that she constantly wore and did her jobs in; instead she was very neat and presentable in a dark skirt and crisp white blouse and flowery apron. She had even gone to the trouble of making up her face. Was he in the right house?

'And another thing, it says an unhappy couple can put people off, so we've to put on an act for half an hour. Manage that, can you?'

He shrugged his shoulders.

'I'm just warning you.'

'I'm warned.'

'Good. And don't get any ideas.'

'About what?'

'Don't think I don't still hate you, you bastard.'

'No sweet nothings, then?'

'Fuck off!'

She flicked the curtain aside to view the drive.

'Anyway, who are these people?' He was annoyed with them already for wanting his house.

'How do I know! The agent sends them round.'

'Didn't he tell you their name.'

'Does it matter?'

'I'd just like to know who'll be crapping in my bog.'

'Omurku.'

'Pardon?'

'Omurku. That's the name.'

'Omurku? That African or something?'

'No idea. You a racist now?'

'God's sake!'

Again she twitched the curtains. Then looked at her watch.

'Fifteen minutes late. Maybe they're not coming. Maybe that hole in the hedge has put them off.'

He avoided her eye.

She looked again.

'Oh ... here they are!' She peered out. 'Don't look African.' Then, peering more intently, 'He's a bit dark, though.'

Turned out they were Irish speakers whose name had been Murphy but was now O'Murchu. Paul hated them on sight. Something about people with passionate convictions. It was as if their very fidelity made them suspect. Conviction and fidelity were words little used in the real world, the happy-go-lucky rugby club milieu he inhabited. If they were spoken at all, it was in hushed tones. You wouldn't want to get a name for that sort of thing.

Anyway, he just knew he didn't want them to have the house. The wife talked to Mary about cooking – a short conversation that one – while the husband, with Paul in tow, walked from room to room tapping walls like a man kicking the tyres of a car he was inspecting. When he actually started kicking the walls, Paul knew it was time for him to go. He casually introduced a story about a very nice neighbour just released after doing life for killing a man he heard speaking Irish. The man hurried off, whispered in his wife's ear; in seconds they were away.

Mary had a suspicious face on her. 'What did you say to him?'

'Nothing.'

'Sure?'

'Sure I'm sure.'

She looked at him. 'Y'know, sometimes I think you don't want this house sold.'

'Why would I want that?'

Was it a trick of the light? Paul looked again. No, Ken was definitely wearing a tie.

'Ah, no!'

'What?' Ken looked sheepish.

'That!'

'What?'

'Frig me!'

'What?'

'That, around your neck!'

'It's a tie.'

'I know it's a tie.'

'So?'

Tony joined in. 'So they've got you at last!'

Ken spun round to face the new attack. 'What?'

Tony laughed. 'The Stepford Wives.'

'Ah, give it a rest, Tony.' He was annoyed.

'An architect with a tie! It's like ... it's like the Venus di Milo with a dick!' said Paul.

A week earlier a memo had been issued from management stating that all staff must conform to a suitable dress code: tie, shirt and suit for men; jacket, blouse and skirt for women. Henceforth there would be a corporate image.

No way! The architects were free spirits; they weren't going to bend to this edict. They didn't want to end up like workers in a Chinese ball-bearing factory. Never! It was beneath their dignity. So they all said at the time. But that was then.

'God's sake, why such a big deal over a bloody tie!' protested Ken.

Paul shared Tony's annoyance. 'Confirms management's

power over us, that's why. They shout, we jump.'

What was worrying was that a month ago Ken was saying the same thing.

Tony gave the tie a tug. 'Badge of the slave, brother!'

Ken shook himself free. 'Bloody union's taken over your brain.'

'At least my neck's my own.'

14

The site proceeded slowly, very slowly. Paul's new-found zeal for perfection meant nothing went smoothly. Everything was a fight, a fight that Paul insisted on winning. It was a knock-out every time. One argument Paul had was about brick sizes. He'd condemned one piece of walling because the vertical joints weren't in line. The brickies complained it wasn't their fault: the bricks weren't a uniform size. He sent Roy to the site to check it out and Roy phoned him to say the bricks were fine; just typical whingeing by the brickies trying to excuse bad workmanship. But later, on site, Danny confirmed the bricks were indeed different sizes, but by then the wall had been knocked down and rebuilt.

'Your mate Roy's bad news round here,' he said. 'They're sayin you back him because you're old rugby mates.'

'Balls!' But there was just enough truth there to hurt. 'Anyway, how'd they know all that about me?'

'Him. Got some mouth on him, yer man. Bad move. All Gaelic fans, the brickies, see. Hate rugby. Anyway, he goes on about how the two of you are drinking together in the clubhouse every Friday night. The lot.'

The eejit! With the sort of people you met with in the building game, you kept your private life to yourself.

'They're right and bitter! Likely the builder won't pay them.'

Later, as he left the site, Paul noticed a large oval shaped chalkmark on the side of Danny's hut that hadn't been there an hour earlier. For all the world just like a rugby ball!

The pub was packed by three o'clock. Red-faced, sweating men jammed slopping pint glasses into each other's chests in an orgy of pre-Christmas cheer, even though the day itself was a month away. Get drunk now and avoid the rush later. The Muzak competed with the buzz of the crowd – and won.

'*Ding-dong merrily on high . . .*'

Paul came in straight from the site. Earlier he'd called with Mary to ask if he could spend one last Christmas in the house. He wasn't quite sure why he wanted to. Anyway she said no. She and Bigmouth and a few friends were going to go to a hotel for Christmas dinner. He was welcome to join them if he liked. He didn't like. His mood was glum, so he was look-ing forward to a few pints. The others had been in since lunchtime and were already up at the bar, talking out of their arses – he'd have to hurry to catch up. Stella was there too; he positioned himself so that he wouldn't have to face her. Val was left in the office in charge of the phones. The squeeze was terrible. Funny what you notice in people up close. Paul had long observed that only happily married middle-aged men have hairs sprouting from their noses and ears; unhappily married ones keep themselves trimmed for the market. Ken and Tony both sported lush foliage; he envied them.

Only noisy architects at the bar. The engineers and quan-tity surveyors held more sedate counsel in the far corner of the lounge. The cause of the gathering was the leaving of one of the engineers, taking early retirement. He'd made a polite, sober farewell speech earlier in the boardroom, which was equally politely and soberly received. But here in the warm, friendly, alcohol-induced atmosphere of the pub, tongues began to loosen. Tony's in particular.

'Well, I thought he was pathetic. Pa-friggin-thetic!'

Paul had succeeded in squeezing through and joining his own group at the front of the bar. Tony, flush-faced, was pronouncing on the occasion.

'Everyone knows he didn't want to go. He's only fifty. He'd another fifteen years in him.'

Paul looked across at the retiree and thought he himself wouldn't mind retiring at fifty. If he lived that long.

'Pa-friggin-thetic! He had his one chance back there to say what he really felt. A speech from the dock. There they all were: Steve, Johnson, the regional architects, the directors, all sitting smiling, thinking there's another one gone. And he didn't bother.'

'How d'you know it doesn't suit him to go?' said Ken.

'Yes, how?' said Stella.

'He told me.'

'Oh. Then why ...'

'Do none of you ever notice anything?'

'What like?' said Ken.

Tony was getting annoyed. 'The poor bugger was off twice with depression. Didn't it occur to anybody to ask why?'

Secretly Paul envied him being off all that time. He thought he wouldn't mind a bit of depression – something light, nothing too heavy like. Might be worth it. Do a bit of circuit training at the club, some gardening, reading, catch up on a lot of those jobs he'd put permanently on the long finger. Not forgetting getting in some serious drinking. And what's more having your pay running all the time! Depression had its upside too.

'Poor man,' said Stella.

'Why'd he go, then?' said Ken.

'His life was made a bloody misery.'

'What by?'said Ken.

'Can't you guess?'

'Y'mean, here? In work?'

'Yes.'

'What, then?' said Stella.

'The system.'

'Market testing?'

'What else! That man was an excellent, conscientious worker. A perfectionist. The system showed that all his jobs were losing money, no matter how hard he worked. Made him feel a failure, a liability. All the time the slipway was being greased for his departure. Another technical post bites the dust.'

Tony looked at the faces around. He had ambitions to rise in the union. One day he hoped to address the annual conference. Good public speaking was an advantage. He had to start somewhere.

'And we've got one of our own to thank – Steve – for leading us into the bloody system.'

Paul used to envy Tony, the way he could just launch into a speech; until Ken told him he caught him practising in the toilet mirror beforehand.

'That Steve is such a creep!' said Stella.

Conversation faltered as they were shunted about by a ripple in the crowd. Pam emerged breathless into their orbit.

'Hi, folks!' She looked at their faces. 'God! Where's the wake?'

'Do we look like a wake?' said Stella.

'No. That's why I'm asking. There'd be more fun at a wake.'

'We've been discussing our future,' said Tony.

'Or the lack of it,' said Ken.

'Oh, spare me! I've been hearing that all day.'

'What?' said Tony.

'Here, will one of you rich architects buy a poor temp a drink? A pint will do nicely.'

Paul stared at her. There was something different about her. She'd made a bit of an effort for the occasion. She'd let down her hair, put on lipstick. Nice tits. She looked – well – attractive. He got a sort of feeling that she was making a play for him.

'I'll get it.' He elbowed Tony aside to get the barman's attention.

'What's this about our future?' Tony persisted.

'Oh, I hear things.'

'What?'

'Things.'

'Pam, quit friggin about!'

'Oh, just bits and pieces, y'know, as I move about. I'm sure they wouldn't want me to betray confidences.'

'But you will?'

'Everyone has his price.'

'And yours?'

She looked around her in mock anxiety. 'That pint here yet?'

'It's ordered. Go on!'

'So what are they saying about us?' said Ken.

'Plenty.'

'Well?'

She leaned into their faces. 'Well, I happened to hear one of the directors on the phone to somebody. He was saying if he could encourage all those architects at the top of their scales – that's the older ones, all you lot – to take early retirement, they could get the same work done by younger, cheaper ones and that would save a lot on the budget.'

'There you have it,' said Tony, drawing back triumph-
antly.

'Bastards!' said Ken.

'Bastards!' agreed Paul.

But he felt a bit of a traitor. The idea of an early retirement
package with a pension and a lump sum had begun to seem
not unattractive to him lately. Life was short. His biblical
span three-quarters way through. Enjoy what there was left
of it while it was there.

'Well, early retirement's no use to me,' said Stella. 'I'm not
here long enough. I'd get a miserable pension. And I've two
kids to bring up.'

'Now hold on!' Ken had his concerned look. 'The union
has an agreement with management that there'll be no com-
pulsory redundancies. Right, Tony?' He was suddenly a fire-
brand for the union. 'So what's to worry about?'

Tony nodded over to the now boisterous engineers
milling about the retiree.

'Over there . . . that's what's to worry about. If they can't
get rid of you one way, they'll find another.'

He turned to Pam. 'Speaking about arseholes . . . how'd
you manage to give him the slip?'

'I didn't. See −' she nodded towards the entrance − 'he's
just come in.'

Tony craned his neck.

'Where? I don't . . . Oh, yes . . .'

Steve was progressing slowly through the crowd in a
bubble of rejection. Animated faces dulled at his approach,
backs were turned, chilly smiles answered his greetings. He
passed across the room like a cold front. Normal service
resumed in his wake.

'I don't believe it! He's going over to yer man!'

They all now strained to look.

'Told me he was,' said Pam. 'He's doing his "sorry-no-hard–feelings–it's–not–me–its–the–system" bit.'

'Neck like brass.'

Suddenly angry voices arose from the engineers' corner. Steve had arrived. But above all, even above the Christmas Muzak, rose that of the retiring engineer – no longer retiring, no longer polite. No longer sober.

'*Ding-dong merrily on high . . .*'

'See you . . . See you . . . y'bastard, yeh!'

'*In Heaven the bells are ringing.*'

Tony could just make out the finger jabbing Steve's chest.

'You're the most hated fucker in this fuckin organisation. D'you know that? Do you?'

'*. . . Full of angels singing . . .*'

'See you . . . the best part of you ran down yer ma's leg! Tell me . . . what's it like to be hated by everybody, eh . . . eh . . . eh?'

They tried to push forward to catch Steve's reply. But it was either nonexistent or too short, for all they were aware of was the crowd parting again as Steve's bubble headed in reverse for the door.

'*Glor- glooooor . . . glooor . . . gloooria!*'

'And good friggin riddance,' said Tony.

'*. . . In Excelsis day . . . ay . . . o!*'

Christmas had arrived early.

15

Silence hung over the site. The brickwork should have been progressing, but wasn't. No machinery moved. Men stood talking quietly in groups. It was like the aftermath of an accident. The word was out that Runian would definitely not be paying for making good the defective brickwork. This was bad news for the brickies; it represented about a week's lost wages for each man in the squad involved. A week of handling rough concrete blocks in cold weather with hands chapped, bleeding and blue with cold – only wimps wore gloves – and all for nothing. They gathered in an angry huddle outside the door of the builder's hut.

Inside, Runian was uneasy. At his meeting with the brickies that morning, he had said that if they didn't start work again within the hour they could gather up their gear and clear off to hell out of his sight. It was up to them. Both he, Maguire and the foreman looked apprehensive as Danny and Paul arrived to start the monthly site meeting. The hour was nearly up.

'Somebody won the lottery?' said Danny as he looked at the glum faces along the table.

The foreman started to smile, but checked with his boss, who wasn't. He resumed the corporate scowl.

Paul laid out his neatly arranged site minutes pro-forma

sheets, with their headings of the various trades and the percentage completions of each at that point in time. He straightened out the sheets on the table before him and laid out his biros on top of them, ready for action. The first item in the minutes, the progress of the works.

'Progress?' Paul intoned the first of the headings.

'Fuck all,' replied Runian.

'Remedial work ongoing to brickwork of ten dwellings might be a better way of phrasing it,' smarmed Maguire.

'Still fuck all as far as I'm concerned. No money in it for me.'

Outside a chainsaw roared into life.

Maguire and the foreman turned. A loud hammering and shouting outside the bolted door. It shook on its hinges.

Runian went white.

'What t'fuck!'

The door burst open and the brickie ganger crashed in with the chainsaw leaping and juddering in his hands like a living thing. He dug it into the end of the table and, barely breaking stride, sliced up the centre, sending the table splaying out in two halves and a bow wave of wood chips over the terrified onlookers on either side. Runian, at the table head, sat transfixed and still as a Buddha as the saw, roaring and whirring, came to rest an inch below his chin.

'About our money, Mr Runian . . .'

'Sambo's gone three days now. I don't think he'll be back.'

Mary stood at the door glaring at him. She crinkled up her eyes. 'Have you got him? Wouldn't put it past you!'

'Me?'

'Tell the truth!'

'I am!'

He didn't invite her in. He wouldn't give her the pleasure of seeing the squalor he was living in. Also, Claire had visited last night and some of her clothes were scattered about – he reckoned she left them on purpose, like marking out her territory.

'Sure?'

'Sure, I'm sure.'

So he was a cat thief now! She never cared that much for Sambo anyway. It was his cat. She held on to Sambo just to spite him. Even letting Bigmouth Ryan come in and feed him. She wouldn't care if the cat disappeared. Probably delighted. This visit was just another chance to hammer him about a bit.

'No. I wouldn't put it past you.'

He ignored the jibe. This was too serious.

'When did you last see him?'

'Three nights ago. I told you.'

Three nights! Sambo was usually in at nights, but when he did go out, he was back first thing next morning, mewing and scrabbling at the window.

'What about Bigmouth Ryan, has he seen him?'

'No. And his name's Jim.'

'Of course. Jim Bigmouth Ryan.'

She started to move away.

'So, did you tell the police or anything?' He wanted to drag it out. He wasn't sure why. Nowadays, outside work, he rarely got speaking to another human being. Single-person syndrome.

'You stupid? A cat! Anyway, haven't I had enough of them over that broken window!'

'Well, I think you should.'

'Police? Catch yourself on! A cat!' As she reached the gate she turned. 'I just thought you ought to know about it, seeing you'd more regard for that animal than you ever had for your wife.'

It shocked him, just coming straight out like that. But –

it had to be faced – it was true, in a way. He didn't know why, but he always seemed to remember Sambo's birthday but never hers. Once, in a rage, she asked what was so special about the cat and he said, 'Well, can you catch mice and lick your own backside?' That started it. But when he apologised later and said he didn't mean both at the one time, that really sent her crazy. Poor sense of humour, women.

Lately the flat seemed lonelier than ever. He'd always hoped Sambo would come to live with him; that Mary would relent. But no. There was a practical point, however. Cats hate moving. Sambo had his runs and his cat friends around there. He'd miss all that. He'd be an exile. He knew that cat; he was an individual, had his own ways. He was different, like him. A cat that refused to be categorised. Or indeed cauterised. When Mary went on about the smell and hinted at having him 'done', he put his foot down. Sambo was a proud, pungent, free-range monument to tomdom, to unfettered promiscuous feline fecundity; he was a machine for converting Whiskas into spermatozoa and noise. He ignored her protestations. Anyway, he'd a sneaking feeling it was an attempt to castrate him at one remove. He remembered she'd even called him a tomcat the time she found the lipstick on his shirt.

But now Sambo was lost, out there somewhere in the dark night, alone, friendless, cold and wet. He couldn't let it rest there. That night he toured the back alleys and gardens around his former house, calling out for Sambo. He got some funny looks. He saw Mary's bedroom light was on. He saw her shape on the blind. He checked Bigmouth's house. His bedroom light was on and he saw the unmistakable silhouette drift across the window.

He was annoyed at himself for thinking the thought. He went away.

★

Mary rang him the next night. He could hear the fear in her voice.

'It's all your fault.'

'What?'

'All this.'

'What?'

'Everything!'

She kept getting these strange calls, she said. But now no longer silent. There was a man's voice, saying the most awful things. Something about a building site.

His ears pricked up. 'What'd he say?'

'Don't understand half it. But it's to do with your stupid old job. I'm telling you right now, I've had a bellyful of this. I'm phoning the police.'

The brickies got paid. Paul heard this from Danny, who knew everything that was happening both on and off the site. The incident with the chainsaw was not mentioned again. To Runian it was a mere bagatelle in a builder's busy life. According to Danny, the saw-wielding brickie was a very serious man. He once had a rival's legs broken for sending his wife a Valentine card – the man's own wife, that is; the brickie was seeing her at the time. And the rival was no soft touch himself. His name was McCann. Pat to his friends; Genghis to his enemies.

And Danny told him of Runian's other worries. The site backed onto the peace line and he'd barely finished fencing it off before he had visits from the patriots from both sides, each gang offering him and his site protection from people exactly like themselves. A grand a month was the going rate for a site that size. Bargain price, he was assured – there was a sale on. Now this was tricky. Runian pointed out to each that while he was willing to pay once, he would not, could not, pay twice. There was an uneasy time while intermediaries moved between the two gangs. First a meeting between lesser lights was set up in a neighbouring pub for talks about talks. Then the more senior hoods came together – via an intermediary – for proximity talks in the same pub. Finally, when faced with the only other option of shooting each other, they agreed to split the spoils. Each gang would collect week about. It was an amicable arrangement, sealed with a bottle of whiskey, before each side returned to their own streets to begin stalking each other again when darkness fell. Runian hated them. But he smiled as he handed over his hard-earned money. He had to; it was the real world he was dealing with. It was that or leave the building game entirely.

Hearing this, Paul almost felt sorry for the builder. But then he thought, why should he? After all, his troubles were mostly of his own making. There was so much work being condemned and pulled down that the site seemed to be going into reverse. All he had to do was to get proper trades-men to produce proper work. He, as architect, certainly wasn't going to compromise on standards. No way. Those days were over. Mr Evil Bastard wouldn't wear it.

Danny had one more interesting titbit. He had heard that Maguire and Johnson were seen playing golf together.

'*Les Liaisons Dangerous*,' he said, with a knowing wink.

Paul was surprised at his breadth of reading.

'Seen it on the TV last night,' he explained.

Tony was in despair. In a contest between the computer and the architects' own estimation of their workload, manage-ment was behind the computer every time. Facts, they said, cannot lie. But then – deliverance; he had a brain wave. It was brought on by a chance remark of Pam, who had contacts at every level and in every department of the organisation. It was a mad idea, but these were desperate times. It was a chance for the architects to arise, phoenix-like, from the ashes of market testing. It had to be tried. Death or glory!

Pam had told him about her friend whose job was to input the architects' production figures into the computer. Recently she had accidentally left out a nought, which immediately showed that all the jobs were non-profit-making. She rectified the mistake with no harm done and without anyone knowing about it. The point was that the process was so complicated and the data to be input so vast and detailed that, other than herself, no one would ever have been aware of the mistake and the whole technical department could have been made redundant because of it.

It occurred to him that had the mistake gone the other way, if an extra nought had been added, the architects' department would soar into profit and all their jobs would be secure. And, after all, it wasn't real money they were talking about here, just numbers in a machine. Morally he would have no objection to shading matters the architects' way; he considered the whole market testing process manipulated anyway. It would only be a matter of levelling the playing field. But would Pam's friend do such a thing? Would Pam ask her?

'No problem.'

'You sure?'

'She's on a year's contract like me. They pay her in buttons, and her with a first in computer studies! So she doesn't give a fuck.'

'The thing is, if it ever gets out, she just says it's a typo. Shit happens.'

'Do anything for a laugh, her.'

'Pam, you're a star.'

16

He'd been avoiding Joan. The memory of 7 Prince Charles Mews was still too fresh or, more accurately, too recent. It clung to him like a wet mist rising off a sewage pond. What a dickhead! He'd wanted her to see him as an ass-kicking Alpha male. He'd wanted to impress her; he'd wanted her to see him showing this unruly but highly esteemed customer who was boss. Instead he ended up creeping away with the dog's tail between his legs. He'd lain doggo ever since.

She phoned a few days later to check that he'd contacted the builder as promised.

He had.

'Must be jokin, mate!' the builder had said. 'Dirty hole, that. Need to send a friggin canary in first. Might get leprosy or the mange in there. Men won't go in till it's cleaned out. I mean, would you?'

Reluctantly he relayed this to Joan.

'Oh dear!' she said.

And then silence.

'Joan?'

'It's just . . .' She sighed. 'It gets nasty now.'

'Sorry.'

'Oh, it's not your fault, Paul.'

He knew it wasn't, but he felt bad anyway. The tenant was housing management's responsibility. It was up to that department to see that the property was available and suitable for the contractor to work in. She would have to arrange to have the place cleaned out before any work could start. He explained this to her.

Again the sigh. 'Oh dear.'

'Sorry.'

'I suppose it means the fumigators?'

'Afraid so.'

She sighed. 'Customers kick up when you send the fumigators in. They hate it. They take it personally.'

Paul couldn't imagine anything more personal than standing up to the ankles in your own excrement.

'Sorry.'

'A slight, that's how they see it. We try not to be too judgemental.'

Judgemental? Surely shitting in your own living room was a stoning-to-death affair.

'It gets worse. Seems he told the builder he won't let anybody else in. Dug his heels in.'

Another long sigh. 'We'll just have to evict if he doesn't let the fumigators in.'

'Not the full shilling, yer man.'

'Whatever. But we can't let that situation remain as it is.'

But there it had remained. Until now.

The first hints of trouble were the sounds of excited female voices coming up the back stairs. The fire doors burst open and the five housing officers crowded in. They headed for Paul. Joan led the charge. Her hair was wild, her face was flushed and she was breathless. She looked stunning.

'Paul, you've got to come down to reception. There's a customer asking for you!'

'Me?'

'Yes. It's Mr Brown.'

'Who?'

'Mr Brown. Remember?'

His face fell. '*The* Mr Brown?'

'I've told him we're there to answer any queries – that's our job. But he said he wants to talk to the architect. He says you're the important man and he doesn't want to be fobbed off!'

His spirits lifted. Possibilities began to appear. He was the man in the big picture now. Here was his opportunity to redeem himself in Joan's eyes, to take a strong hand with the shite monster. A second chance. An Alpha male at last. There was a God! But . . .

'Is the dog there?'

'No,' she said.

He started up. He was full of fight. He'd go down there and he'd . . .

'There's just one thing . . .'

He sat down again. There had to be a catch.

'He's got two plastic bags with him . . .' She hesitated.

He stood up again.

'. . . full of . . . full of . . .'

'Shite . . .' interjected one of the lower grades helpfully.

He sat down again. His desire for combat wilted.

'Yes, that. He says he's going to empty them over your head!'

The case against going down was strengthening by the minute.

'Nobody else will do. He insists on seeing you, Paul. He's a really awful man.'

The others nodded in wide-eyed confirmation. They all looked at him. The helpful one was now going around the drawing office, telling everyone that a customer with a bag of shite was running amok in the reception hall. Stella, Ken and Tony grimaced at the less than delicate announcement. Val was on the point of fainting. Everyone in the room was looking at him. Pam had now joined the gawping multitude. But he didn't care; he was the centre of attention – Joan's attention – and it felt good. Suddenly nothing else mattered.

Joan appealed to him with her eyes. 'We don't want to ... y'know ... phone the police if we can possibly ... y'know ...'

'Oh, no, of course not,' Paul agreed helpfully. But he didn't really agree. Personally he'd call in the SAS with flame-throwers.

'Mr Johnson feels it would be ... y'know ... bad PR.'

'Of course,' he agreed again. But then why wasn't Johnson himself down facing the shite monster?

'So I thought ... I thought ... if you could possibly ...' She trailed off as she saw him rise.

'No problem, Joan.'

He squared his shoulders and made for the door. This was his moment. He was Gary Cooper in *High Noon*, John Wayne in *True Grit*, Alan Ladd in *Shane*.

'Do be careful, Paul. I'm sure he's not all there.'

Warmed by these words, he went down the back stairs. He was a knight blessed by his lady before setting out to slay the dragon. With the beautiful Joan caring for him, what was there to fear? Anyway, God had given him this second chance to shine in her eyes. He wasn't going to mess it up.

The reception area was empty – almost. And quiet. Normally it was full of mothers and young children and buggies, all cocooned in a fug of cigarette smoke and wailing. And there was always a faint whiff of urine and baby cream which the aroma of cheap scent and BO couldn't quite subdue. But not today. Today there was another more pungent odour, an odour that emanated from the solitary figure standing defiantly at the counter, arms extended, with a bulging plastic bag dangling from each, for all the world like the figure of justice on top of the courthouse. A security man holding his nose hovered uneasily in the background.

Humour him. Put him at his ease. That was the way.

'Can I help you, Mr Brown?' It occurred to him how apt the man's name was.

Mr Brown smiled. It wasn't a happy smile. He squeezed his eyes tight in a short-sighted inspection.

'The very man!'

Paul smiled an uneasy smile back.

'The archeeteck has all the answers, right?'

'Well . . .'

'So, where'll I put this shite, then, Mr friggin Archeeteck?' He shook the bags teasingly. 'See, there's nowhere in my house. I've no toilet. But you know that.'

He started to swing the two plastic bags out in front of him like incense.

A touch of sternness needed.

'Mr Brown, three times a plumber called and . . .'

'I told yous, I want no fenian plumbers in my house! Understand?'

'But the builder . . .'

'Fuck the builder. You're the boss. I wanna protestant plumber or else I'll . . .'

'I can't tell the builder who to hire!'

'You're the friggin archeeteck! You shout, they jump.'

'No, you're wrong, Mr Brown. See, the contract says . . .'

The man's eyes narrowed. 'Oh, I know. I know. I get it now . . .' His finger jabbed across the distance at Paul. 'You're one o'them too! Right?'

This was getting ridiculous.

'Mr Brown . . .'

'An' that's why you're on that site the other side of the

wall. Am't I right? Yous all stick together. I'm not blind, y'know. You just watch yerself, boy. That's all I'm sayin.'

Unreason had taken over. Time to leave.

'Oh, by the way,' the man said, 'this is for you.'

With that, he began twirling one of the plastic bags around his head. Forewarned, Paul ducked low. And instead of peppering his enemy, the contents of the bag slipped out and slithered over the man's own head and shoulders, then down his body onto the ground. He looked down at himself.

'Aw . . . fuck's sake!'

He attempted to swing the other bag before his quarry, now moving fast, got out of range. But his foot slipped on the contents of the first bag, and that of the second – now equally out of control – again cascaded over his head and shoulders as he hit the floor with a squelch.

In a flash the security man was onto him, trapping him on the floor with a chair as he slithered aimlessly. No hands-on job, this. But he squirmed out from under it and got to his feet. The security man backed off, brandishing the chair in front of him like a lion tamer. But Mr Brown didn't even notice him. He just stood looking down at himself.

'Aw, fuck's sake! Fuck's sake!'

Shaking his head, he walked to the exit, dung-covered arms held well away from his body, a mobile crucifixion scene minus the cross. The crowd of open-mouthed and clenched-nostriled onlookers outside parted before him. With one hand on the door, he turned and pointed a finger at Paul.

'See you! You're dead!'

Paul went back upstairs. Victory was his. Now he would claim his prize. Now he would tell Joan to fear no more: the shite monster had been vanquished. By him.

But she wasn't there.

The other housing officers were. They hailed him as the hero of the hour. But it was Joan he wanted to tell him that. He had to make do with Pam.

'So you're a real man, then!'

He waited for the barb. There was none.

'Surprised?' he said.

'Just . . . aren't many about.'

He was looking around him as she talked, looking past her to the left, to the right. Looking for Joan. She swung her face to obstruct his view. Games again.

'Know where Joan went?'

'Pardon?'

'Joan. Do y'know where . . .'

'Heard you the first time.'

'What?'

'She was called up to Johnson's office.' She narrowed her eyes. 'Why?'

'Oh, nothing.'

'You consorting with the enemy, then?'

'What's that mean?'

'You fancy her?'

'What!'

'Just want into her knickers, don't you?'

'Frig's sake!'

'Be honest!'

'No,' he lied.

'Seriously?'

'Seriously.'

She looked at him. 'You queer?'

'Pam!'

'I won't tell anybody. Honest!'

'No. I'm not.'

'You bloody do fancy her.'

'Look, this is stupid.'

She tilted her head to the side to study his reaction. 'Steve has the hots for me, y'know . . .'

As if he cared! No doubt about it: she was jealous!

'Of course, he's the hots for anything in a skirt. I play up to him, show a bit of cleavage, wiggle the bum. Oh, he watches all right, the dirty brute.'

'Why do you do it?'

'Gives me a laugh.'

Then the biggest surprise of all. She began to let him into the secrets of her work day. Being a general gofer, she had access to places where Paul – or indeed any of the architects – rarely if ever went. She seemed to know everything that was going on, had her ear to the ground, had contacts in every department. She learned of board decisions before even the directors. She liked to be on the inside track, ahead of the field. She saw him wondering how she did it.

'A pleasant smile and a neck as hard as a jockey's bollocks will get you anywhere,' she said sweetly.

And she did go anywhere, could be seen anywhere. No one minded her flying about. Behind a giddy exterior she was bright and streetwise, but took great care to hide the fact. She was frequently up in the rarefied atmosphere of the sumptuously carpeted fifteenth floor. Here she would leave reports in the boardroom for upcoming meetings. As the directors met to consider these only once a month, the room was generally unoccupied. The double doors to the boardroom were purposefully imposing and no one would just casually walk in. A diary outside told who had booked the room and when, so it was quite easy to ensure when it was free. She would come here at times to read the paper for jobs, taking her ease in the deep embrace of the leather armchairs.

All this Paul took in with growing respect.

'The boardroom's free now. Wanna have a look?'

Against his better judgement, but because she was doing the architects a favour, he decided to humour her.

As she showed him around, she became quite proprietorial.

'Here. What d'you fancy?'

She opened an unlocked cocktail cabinet to reveal an array of bottles: whiskey, brandy, vodka, gin, some beers, wine, assorted mixers and glasses; even nuts and crisps. The directors looked after themselves well. Many of the bottles had been opened. She selected two glasses and poured each of them a vodka, then added a dash of orange.

'I top them up with a drop of water every so often. They never notice. Here!'

It felt strange drinking in the boardroom, the holy of holies. Almost sacrilegious. After a few sips it seemed less so.

'You've done this before?'

She winked. 'Haven't you noticed? I'm half pissed most of the time.'

'Y'serious?' He was impressed.

'How else d'you think I could stick this boring job!'

She showed him the rest of her domain: the directors' private shower room and toilet, the small kitchen for snacks, the trouser press. She often showered here in hot weather; and when she felt like it, she'd make herself lunch. She always removed any traces of her visits and had gotten away with it to date. Once she had encountered two cleaners, but she carried herself with such a confident air that they assumed she was someone of substance.

'Our secret, OK?'

'Not a word.'

'You can come up here yourself sometime. Get your head down, have a shower, whatever. I'd give you the all clear.'

He laughed. 'This is crazy.'

'Seriously. Why not?'

'Might,' he lied. He wasn't as mad as her.

They took the lift down again to the uncarpeted lower floors. The vodka he'd had made him feel sleepy. He'd no wish to breathe fumes over Ken, so he signed himself out to the site – but went home instead. It was the first time he'd done that. He was surprised at himself. His standards were starting to slip.

17

Sambo. He was ashamed to admit that he'd almost forgotten about the cat. Two weeks gone and no word. Then.

'Well, what do you make of that?'

Mary stood on his doorstep. She held out a photo. It was a Polaroid close-up of Sambo with the day before's *Irish News* front page as a backdrop.

'Arrived this morning. Wasn't addressed to anybody.'

He looked at it. 'Bloody hell!' He turned it around. 'Any message or anything?'

'Nothing.'

It was the same old Sambo, looking self-satisfied as usual, staring straight into the camera.

'I thought it might be some of your rugby club ones playing a trick.'

Never. Rugby types would never do the like of that. They might tie a can to a cat's tail, or shave it – the deeper thinkers among them – but to keep a cat for two weeks required a commitment beyond most.

'Bloody hell!' he said again.

There were no likely culprits, nobody that twisted to keep a cat that long. Weird. But the more he looked at the photo, the more it dawned on him what it reminded him of: the Beirut hostages.

'He's been catnapped.'

'What?'

'It's obvious.'

'Don't be silly!'

'What else? Some sicko.'

'But who would want a cat?'

'Apart from another cat? Not many.'

'Be serious. I'm scared.'

He hated to see her scared. But it had to be faced: Sambo had become the Brian Keenan of the cat world.

'You're not backing us, then?'

Paul, who had suggested not filling in time sheets any more, accompanied Tony to see Sam, the union rep. They had decided some sort of protest had to be made. It was time the union did something for them; not that they held out much hope from that quarter, but they had to be seen to be going through the motions.

Sam's face fell at their approach. He had an idea what was coming: the market-testing exercise was creating mayhem throughout the organisation. He was weary of it all. He did his best to field the fusillade of complaints and queries that had been landing on him since it had begun. He suspected Tony was about to add to the assault.

He was. The architects had agreed on this final action before giving the go-ahead for fixing the computer input. It was one of those confrontations that was painful for both. Tony, on behalf of the membership, was asking a question to which he already knew the answer.

'Can't, Tony. It's one the union couldn't win. You can see that.'

Sam resented Tony for putting him in the position of having to say no. He liked the union to present a positive, modern accommodating image. Only questions requiring the answer 'yes' were welcome.

'Not filling in the time sheets could be viewed as a breach of contract – and they could sack you. Nobody wants that. You don't want that.'

Of course he didn't. But he had to be seen to be doing something; the members were restless. The architects were lukewarm at best about union membership. The older ones particularly were uneasy at being lumped together with the cloth-cap and lunch-box masses; they were professionals after all. Some of them were just looking for an excuse to jump ship: people like Ken. There were times Paul wished he was like Ken; life was much simpler when you just did what you were told. The joys of being a toerag: no confrontations, no anxiety. No balls required.

He had a good idea that the union wouldn't back them. Tony knew this as well, but he just didn't want to be seen to succumb too easily.

'Y'see our problem, don't you?' said Tony. 'The time sheets make us look loss-making. I mean ... how can you measure a public service? We're not just sitting here churning out so many friggin ball bearings per day. We're dealing with the public, with feelings, with sensitivities. How do you measure that! When our time sheets go into that computer, we're feeding the monster that'll devour us!'

Sam nodded. But he'd heard it all before. Much as he sympathised, he couldn't stop his eyes from glazing over.

'See, if they can show we're making losses, it means we have to take on more work just to stay still, and we're already snowed under. Understand?'

Sam jerked himself back to wakefulness. 'Sure. Sure.' Tony's eyes boring into him wouldn't let him slip away into the unconsciousness both of them knew he yearned for.

'It's a treadmill. Like, how do we protect ourselves from the stress of it all? This could be a striking matter. It's a health issue. Stress kills, y'know.' He thought this might energise the slumping Sam. It did.

He sat up suddenly, his face alight with revelation. 'Hey ... there's an idea! You've given me an idea.'

Tony looked at him. He leaned forward eagerly.

Even Paul brightened. Was there another way after all? To tell the truth, he felt uneasy about fiddling the computer, and nobody wanted to risk a strike, least of all him. God, no. With a divorce pending and two households to maintain, he was keen to hold on to his salary.

Sam too leaned forward. His eyes locked onto theirs, turn about, as he paused before delivering himself of his inspiration.

'Serious ... illness.'

He pronounced each word separately and deliberately, then leaned back and gave a satisfied sigh, as if he had just given birth to the idea of the century.

Paul and Tony looked at each other.

'What about it?' said Paul.

'Have you got one?'

'One what?'

'Something ... anything brought on by stress at work, that sorta thing?'

'No,' said Tony. 'Not yet anyway.

Paul was on the point of offering his raised blood pressure, but it didn't seem ambitious enough for Sam's expectations.

'No,' he said.

'Oh.' Sam slumped back into his chair, a deflated balloon. He looked at them as if they'd just lost a winning lottery ticket. 'Sure now?' He really wanted to help them out. 'Cancer?' he offered hopefully. 'Heart trouble? ... Even a nervous breakdown could put you in the winner's enclosure?'

They just looked at him in silence.

'Pity.' He sank back into his chair.

Paul couldn't believe what he was hearing.

'We could take a bundle off them for that, y'know. Happening all over now. Claims for stress-related illnesses brought on by structural change in an organisation. You'd have been on a winner there, boys. On the pig's back.'

Paul shook himself. Terminal illness as a sharp career move – now why hadn't he thought of that? Stupid or what!

Sam pushed himself further back in his chair with the exasperated air of one who had just made a killer point which was obviously beyond the intellectual capacity of his opponent.

He stared at Tony's nonplussed face. 'You sure now? Nothin? Doesn't even have to be actually life-threatening or – Hey, hey, boys . . . where you goin?'

18

Normally the architects' monthly performance reports, based on their time sheets, fulfilled the function of a dartboard; they certainly weren't read by the people they purported to examine. They were a haze of minute print and graphs incomprehensible to all except those in the computer department who compiled them. Today, however, they were viewed with intense interest.

'Thought you knew that's what they were doing?' Pam sat on Tony's desk, swinging her legs and munching an apple.

'Well, I didn't,' said Ken.

'It's all there in the monthly reports.' She flicked the core expertly across the room, landing it in Ken's waste bin with a satisfying ping.

Ken bridled – not at the uninvited invasion of his waste bin, but because this mere gofer apparently understood the mass of data in the report. He certainly didn't.

'We don't read that rubbish,' said Tony, who hadn't a clue either.

'We use our time for real work,' said Paul. Ditto.

'So how do you expect to know what's going on?'

She herself then proceeded to inform them. Through her contacts she had discovered that what paper profits there were from their jobs were being creamed off and put into a separate management budget, pushing them even further out along the loser's gangplank. And flushed with their consequently increased budget, management was currently recruiting three new admin people to further monitor the architects' work.

'So you guys will have to work harder to pay for more people to watch you working even harder to pay for even more people to watch ... etc, etc. Neat, eh?' She smiled pleasantly, looking around to see if anyone else appreciated the machiavellian beauty of it all.

Ken was outraged. 'But there'll be more admin people monitoring the architects than there are architects. Doesn't make sense!

'Does if you're an admin person,' said Pam. 'Ever hear of empire building?'

'Well, that's it,' said Tony, standing up. He could hear the drum rolls, the trumpets calling. The time for talking was over.

They looked at him.

'It's the nuclear option. No other choice.'

19

The voice was familiar.

'Paul, I'm sorry to ring you at work, but I don't have your new phone number.'

'Who is this?'

'It's Jim.'

Jim? Jim?

'Who?'

'Jim Ryan.'

It took him a few seconds to take this in.

Bigmouth!

'You're probably surprised to hear from me . . .'

And how! He'd hardly talk to him if he met him on the street.

'What's up?' He was alarmed now.

'Oh, nothing. Nothing, Paul. It's just . . . Mind you, Mary doesn't know I'm ringing you . . .'

What was he on about?

'She probably wouldn't want me to . . . You know how she is . . . Well, of course you do . . . you being her husband and everything . . .'

'What are you trying to say?'

There was silence for a bit. Then:

'I'm asking you to stop, Paul.'

'Stop what?'

'Stop ringing her.'

Had he heard right?

'You want what?'

'I know it's you, those strange phone calls, and I want you to stop, 'cause it's wrecking her.'

He had heard right.

'I even saw you cruising by her house the other night. I . . . I care about her, Paul. Even if you don't.'

Was this man talking about his ex- (almost) wife? He thought of all the things he could say, he should say.

He slammed the phone down.

Steve took his job very seriously indeed. Previously, like all the architects, he was made to feel that he was merely on the fringe of events, clinging to the periphery of the organisation. Now he *was* the organisation – an insider at last. And with this came an awareness of a global responsibility. Now he saw his duty as extending not merely to the elements that he controlled within his own limited sphere of PR operations but to every department and facet of the organisation. What harmed one, harmed all.

Skiving was his particular hate. It was the disloyalty of it that annoyed him, the lack of commitment it revealed. He had decided to mount his own personal crusade against it. Of course, this was properly the territory of the personnel department and individual managers, but he would help them by making it his business to report any abuses that he happened to come across – the equivalent of a citizen's arrest. It wasn't that he himself had never nipped out for a bit of shopping on the sly, but that was in the past. Now, with market testing and with every minute having to be accounted for and costed, time was indeed money – and skiving was theft.

So when he encountered Stella coming out of Marks & Sparks laden with shopping bags at half ten in the morning, he tasted blood. He himself was on his own legitimate errand and he slowed his pace to make sure she saw him. She did, and tried to scurry past with not a hint of acknowledgement.

He got a particular pleasure out of this moment. A stuck-up bitch was Stella. She had gone for the same job as him and had never forgiven him for getting it. She'd hardly spoken to him since. Well, now he had her in his power and he could tell by her face that she knew it.

'Nice day, Stella!' he called out to her, looking meaningfully at his watch.

She hurried on.

Paul glowered at the brickies. He couldn't prove anything, but he was sure it was them. The fear on Mary's face, the smashed window, the phone calls – must be them. Who else?

He consoled himself that all this was the price of making a stand; but then, he wasn't the one paying for it. He didn't tell Mary of his suspicions. Didn't want to alarm her even more; and anyway they were only suspicions.

As his anger against the brickies grew, he found his new robust approach to the site liberating. The stress was gone. So it was true: evil bastards must indeed live longer. No more knotted stomachs. No more feeling pain at the brickies' wounded faces as he dithered on the edge of a decision whether or not to demolish two days of their work. From now on it was either right or it was wrong – and to hell with them!

The phone rang.

'Architects' department,' he said.

No voice at the other end. In the background the rasping

of machinery.

'Danny?'

The cautionary pause. Then:

'Right,' came the familiar voice.

'What's up?'

'It's a bollox.'

'What?'

'That corbelling detail.'

'What about it?'

'They're makin a pig's arse of it.'

The brick corbelling band above the ground-floor windows and at the eaves was Paul's little touch. It gave a characterful lift to what would have been an otherwise drab façade.

'But it's on the drawing: alternating courses of red, black and yellow. What's the problem?'

'I've got them to take it down twice already.'

'Taken down twice!'

Out of the corner of his eye he saw Ken paying attention.

'Colours in the wrong order or what?'

'Everythin wrong with it.'

'Well, it'll have to be done right.'

Ken was now at his side. 'More delay, Paul?' He pulled a face.

Paul ignored him. 'Get on to it right away, Danny.'

Ken bustled in. 'Hold on there!' He reached out his hand, jiggling his fingers for the phone.

Paul pretended not to understand. Ken took the phone roughly out of his hand anyway.

'Hello, Danny. Ken here. Paul was telling me about the corbelled brick detail.'

Paul glared at him.

'What sort of a delay we talking about here?'

Paul strained to hear Danny's reply, but couldn't.

'Thing is, we can't afford any more delays on this job. It's costing us.'

Ken swung round, putting his hand over the mouthpiece and whispering to Paul.

'What you say we just forget that detail and do it in plain brickwork?'

Before Paul could reply, Ken swung back and uncovered the mouthpiece.

'Danny, just had a word with Paul. We think maybe it'd be better all round if we just scrub that detail. Yes, let them carry on in plain brickwork. A lot less trouble and hassle. OK?'

He put down the phone and turned to Paul. He shook his head. 'The accountants are getting worried about this job.'

'Accountants!' Paul looked at him.

'Yes ... Johnson's on my back as it is. See, you'd just worry what the directors make of all these loss-making jobs. Rightly or wrongly, it reflects on us.'

He searched Paul's face for agreement. He expected it. He was the boss after all.

There was none.

'Whatever you say, Ken.'

'Accountants dictating our designs! No way!' Tony blazed with indignation. He'd go straight to the union. He'd see something was done about this.

Paul wasn't impressed. Tony meant well, but nothing ever seemed to emerge from his harrying of the union; it was a black hole into which all grievances were sucked, never to be heard of again. Nor did Tony himself seem to expect it. It was almost as if he feared the responsibility of success. He was like a dog chasing a bus – what to do with it if he caught it?

'See what's happening, can't you? It's the accountants

deciding what we design now! And Ken's just going along with it.'

'Well . . .' Paul hesitated at such a sweeping denunciation. 'Seems to be the case, all right. I'm surprised at Ken.'

But he wasn't really.

20

It still rankled that Joan had just disappeared the day he vanquished the shite monster, and with never a word since. He'd done it for her after all! Didn't King Arthur get his Guinevere; John Wayne his Maureen O'Hara? What was wrong with him! She could at least have thanked him.

He knew she took her job seriously, and when Johnson called they all had to jump. But still. According to Pam, Joan seemed to be the main link between Johnson and housing management, and seemed always to be at his beck and call. Once he thought he glimpsed her sprinting up the back stairs, but by the time he got to the landing she had disappeared only the faint trail of her scent hinted at her passing. There was always a lot of toing and froing between Johnson and the housing management people. The architects in between were rarely visited by either. And they were happy to keep it like that.

All except Paul. He turned hopefully at every footfall, willing it to be Joan. He was screwing up his courage to ask her for a date. He could ring her of course, but he held back. What if it went wrong? What if she refused? What if she thought he was too old for her? He wouldn't be able to look her in the eye again. Ever. But they'd still have to work together. No, he wouldn't phone; he'd made up his mind on that. Their next meeting would have to arise naturally. And he didn't want anybody to know. It would be their secret.

'There's your girlfriend!'

Pam was craning her neck out of the car window. She was getting bored in the office all day; she wanted a change. At her insistence, Paul had started to take her out to the site to let her see the reality of what they were dealing with. She enjoyed the banter of the countrymen and gave as good as she got. She said she was partial to the odd flash of builder's bum, a commodity in short supply in the office – except, of course, at Christmas party time. But then architect's arse didn't have quite the same cachet.

'Which one? I've dozens,' he said. But he'd already spotted her himself.

The car was just about to enter the office car park when he saw her, striding along with her tasteful business suit and briefcase. She turned into a café entrance, and he caught a glimpse of someone greeting her there and leading her inside, a hand familiarly on her arm. A man? Yes, but he couldn't see whom. Looked a bit like Johnson. Maybe a relative? A boyfriend perhaps? He was instantly jealous.

Pam nudged him. 'Seen enough?'

He looked at her. 'Who said anything about a girlfriend?'

'Ah, but you'd like her to be.'

'Says who?'

'G'won. Tell the truth!'

'None of your business.'

She smiled. Then, after a silence, 'You've no chance there, y'know.'

'What?'

'I'd say she has her own plans, that one.'

'And what's that mean?'

She shrugged her shoulders. 'Just.'

'Just what?'

'Those housing management types aren't interested in architects. You boys are beaten dockets. You're going nowhere – except down the tubes. And as for married ones . . . Zilch!'

'Know it all, don't you?'

'Not interested in losers, her type.'

'Is that me?'

'Sorry. But true. It's single young fellas with big cars and yachts she's interested in.'

He laughed. 'You think people are that mercenary?'

'I am.' She smiled sweetly as she turned to get out of the car. 'Life's a shite sandwich – the more bread the better. Think about it . . . Makes sense, doesn't it?'

Ryan's house was just seven doors down from Mary's, so Paul decided to make the one trip do two visits. He was going to have it out with him. That phone call annoyed him. Who did he think he was, interfering between man and ex- (almost) wife!

He was knocking Ryan's door and ringing the bell for several minutes without result when Mary, seeing him from her own bedroom window, put down the Kango hammer and signalled to him.

'What are you doing there?'

'Friends are for visiting.'

'Very funny. He's out, well.'

There was an embarrassed silence. A stand-off. There was nobody about in the street, but he felt eyes behind every twitching curtain.

Mary cracked first. 'Suppose you may as well come in now you're here.'

It was odd being in his own sitting room again. In his

favourite chair. He wondered if Bigmouth was ever in it.

'What you want Jim for? Thought you can't stand him.'

'I can't.'

'Well?' She was busy sandpapering a piece of skirting board as she talked. Never wasted a second.

'He thinks it's me making those phone calls?'

'And is it?' She stopped sandpapering and looked up.

'Christ's sake, Mary!'

'Stranger things have happened.'

'Has he told you?'

'No.' She resumed sandpapering.

'Does he be in here much?'

She looked up again. 'This an interrogation?'

'Just curious.'

'Hardly any of your business now, is it?'

That stopped him. He changed tack.

'Any sign of Sambo?'

'Not a whisker.'

'That meant to be funny?'

'Grow up, Paul! It's only a bloody cat!'

'It's Sambo.'

A card on the mantelpiece caught his eye. Printed on it in large letters was MORTUARY ATTENDANTS' ANNUAL BALL. He looked closer. It was an invitation for two. He lifted it.

'This from him?'

'From his wife actually – his ex-wife. She keeps in touch. They've an amicable divorce. All very civilised. He even likes her new man, the mortuary attendant. Says he's really interesting. They go out together sometimes, the three of them.' She squinted up from her sandpapering. 'It's her new man's works' annual bash. She thought Jim might like to go and bring somebody with him.'

'You going?'

'You never know.'

He couldn't believe this! 'You're going with Bigmouth?'

She sighed. 'I didn't say that. If you must know, Jim left it in case you and I wanted to go.'

'Us?'

'Us. Personally, I'd rather have root canal treatment without anaesthetic.'

'Oh, thanks!'

'Thought he was doing us a favour. Get us together. The poor eejit!'

'The mortuary attendants' ball! Very fitting!'

'Still. Nice of him.'

'Wouldn't be seen dead in it!'

'Very funny.'

He felt himself getting angry. 'You're not seriously thinking . . .'

'Didn't say I was going, did I? Anyway, is it any worse than you driving up some country lane with one of your sluts from the rugby club?'

A low blow. And unjust. Slags maybe; not sluts.

'What are you talking about?'

He hoped his note of outrage sufficiently masked his unease. How did she know? What had she heard? But anyway, in the circumstances, what did it matter now?

He banged the door as he left.

21

That night the rugby club beer tasted stale and the jokes from Roy's joke-book repertoire fell similarly flat.

'Daddy, there's a man at the door with a bald head. Tell him to go away, I've got one already!'

Roy's roaring.

'Hear the one about the contortionist who died in his own arms?'

More roars and slapping of thighs. It was all beginning to grate.

Paul was unsettled. The club wasn't the sanctuary from the everyday world it always had been. Something here was getting at him. It was only when Roy started to talk about buying a Saab and moving into his new luxury bungalow at Cultra that he knew what it was: resentment. It had been building up. Lately, every time he thought of Roy he felt the tension, the quickened heartbeat, the pounding blood. He had to get release. Doctor's orders.

'Those bricks, Roy . . .'

'Huh?'

'The bricks on Runian's job . . .'

Roy looked at him in amazement. 'Bricks!'

'Yeah. Runian's job . . .'

Roy laughed and slammed Paul across the shoulders.

'You're jokin! Christ's sake, man, don't talk to me about work! Can't you see I'm enjoying myself . . .'

And he was, red face glistening with sweat as he roared at his own jokes.

'After five o'clock, "work" is the only four-letter word I can't abide in my presence.'

'But it's important –'

Roy raised an outstretched arm, palm upturned, traffic policeman style.

'Now, Paul!'

'Look. It's . . .'

'No! No!' Roy shook his head. 'I won't have it! Get thee behind me, Satan!' He tried to put his hand over Paul's mouth, laughing and looking around, wanting others to enjoy the scene.

What had been simmering in Paul now bubbled over. He pushed the hand away.

'Will you fuck off, Roy!'

Heads turned. Conversation stilled.

'Hey!' Roy looked at him in amazement.

'Different story when you're touting for new orders! You'll talk, then, all right.'

That was it. It was out. The boil lanced. The Rubicon crossed. The bridges burnt.

'What?'

Roy looked stunned. Hurt. A stillness settled around the bar.

'Sure, I'm only jokin, Paul! What's rattled your cage?' He laughed. Nervously.

Paul's mind suddenly flooded with cage rattlers: the batch of odd-coloured bricks that didn't quite match what was already there; the load of bricks that, he later learned, had been rejected on another site as substandard and dumped on him; brick deliveries delayed because other sites were getting priority; and now bricks of different sizes. All these he had let go, because he didn't want to fall out with his old pal Roy. But the resentment simmered. Roy obviously saw him as a soft touch. It hurt. He'd used him, and he allowed himself to be used. What did this say about their friendship? What did it say about Roy? More importantly, what did that say about him?

'Now look, Paul . . . I saw those bricks . . . and yes, OK, the joints in the walls were a bit here and there . . .'

'It was like vertical crazy-paving, that's what it was!' snapped Paul.

'Ah, now, Paul!'

Roy looked round nervously at the worried alicadoos. Angry voices were never heard in the club. Wasn't playing the game, this.

'From now on I'll be using somebody else's bricks,' said Paul.

Roy's mouth fell open. 'Wha. . .'

'You heard.' He was starting to enjoy this.

Roy stared at him. 'Y'know what you're saying, Paul? This could cost me my job. Fuck's sake, I've just taken out a huge mortgage!'

Paul stood up and started to walk away.

'Hey! I'm your pal, remember!'

Paul turned and gave him a look. 'I can buy one like you every day of the week.' He surprised himself. Didn't think he had that in him.

'What!' Roy looked stricken. He stood still for a moment. A lonely figure in a room of silent, averted faces.

Then slowly a smile began to twitch at the corner of his mouth, uncertain at first, then more confident. Then radiant. He started to laugh. Roared laughing. A leg-pull, that's what it was! Of course it was. He beamed his lighthouse smile around the room, encouraging the slack-jawed onlookers to share the joke.

'See you, Paul . . . you're one evil bastard!'

Paul looked back.

Roy, tears of laughter squirting from his eyes, staggered about holding his side and slapping his thigh. He hadn't laughed so much since he had the brain scan in Ballymena.

22

Maguire was on the ball. As soon as he received Paul's written instruction regarding the change in the brick corbelling detail – an exercise which involved less time and fewer materials and therefore less money – he sent in a two-page letter detailing how the change would in fact cost almost as much as previously, what with interruption of supplies, reordering difficulties, head office overheads, general buggeration, etc. It was a masterclass in obfuscation.

Paul showed the letter to Ken.

'Maguire!' Ken smiled and wagged his head appreciatively. 'He's one friggin gangster!'

'We just carry on as before, then?' said Paul.

Ken looked up from the letter. 'What?'

'If it's almost the same price not to have it as to have it, then surely . . .'

Ken put the letter down.

'You're missing the point, Paul.'

'I must be.'

He shook his head, as if dealing with a child. 'See . . . I've told you the directors have their eyes on this job. We have to be seen to be making savings here.'

'But the way Maguire's done his sums we're saving nothing!'

'Now, there is a bit of a saving there.'

'Pennies!'

'Doesn't matter. It's a saving.'

'What?'

Ken looked into the bemused face.

'It's the principle. Just a game, see. As long as we're seen to be taking steps – that's all that counts. We've played our part. We've got some savings – not much, I grant you – but we've jumped through the hoops. We've maybe saved a bit of time into the bargain. Got it? Just a game. Everybody's happy.'

Paul stared at him.

'Don't worry about it!' Ken smiled into the uncomprehending face. 'All just a paper exercise for the accountants.'

'But it's not.'

'Not what?' An edge was creeping into Ken's voice. Why couldn't Paul see what was obvious to all!

'What happens on site isn't just paper . . .'

'What?'

'It's reality I'm dealing with, bricks and mortar reality.'

'I know. I know. But . . .'

'Those houses will be as plain as brick shithouses without that corbelling detail!'

'And that's good enough for what's going into them, if you ask me.' He sniggered, but stopped when he noticed Paul wasn't.

'I was born in a council house,' said Paul.

A lie. But it was worth it just to see Ken's face.

'In bed those two.' Danny sowed the seed of doubt.

'Who?' said Paul.

'Runian and your man.'

'Who?'

'*Your* man.'

'My man?'

'Your boss.'

'Ken?'

'Didn't you know?'

'No.'

'Swear to God!'

'You're jokin!'

'No joke. Brickie told me. Runian built an extension for him a while back. A freebie. Twenty grand's worth.'

'Jesus!' Paul was shocked.

'Nice one, ay?'

'It's unethical!'

'It's free.'

'God!'

'Makes you think, doesn't it?'

'About what?'

'That corbelling detail.'

'What?'

'I'm sayin nothin.'

There was a time lapse for Paul to catch up. Danny was understanding that way.

'Ah, no ... you don't mean ...'

'I'm sayin nothin.'

'God!'

'I'm just sayin.'

'Ken wouldn't do that!'

'You scratch my back. Happens all over.'

'God!'

'Sure there's a lot o'them at it.'

'Who?'

'Architects.'

Paul leaped to the defence of his profession. 'Well, I'd never do it.'

Danny shrugged. 'Takes all kinds.'

Paul looked at him. 'Would you?'

Danny thought for a bit. 'A twenty-grand freebie? Let's face it . . . it's better than a poke in the eye with a pointy stick.'

Paul laughed. 'Of course you wouldn't!' He was willing the reply he wanted.

Danny didn't oblige. He attempted a sly smile. It didn't suit him.

But the talk had brought Paul to a decision.

'Danny, tell the brickies we're back to where we were.'

'You're goin ahead with it?'

'As designed.'

'And what about . . .'

'What?'

'Your boss?'

'Ken? To hell with him!'

As he drove out of the site, Paul noticed a chalked outline of a cat on a newly built brick gable that he had just ordered demolished.

Pam, en route between admin and registry, had just had her mid-morning vodka and was carefully adding just the right amount of water to the depleted bottle when she heard the voices approaching the boardroom door. In a flash she closed the cocktail cupboard and raced into the shower room. This wasn't right. She'd checked the room diary, there were no meetings for this morning. Must be an urgent special. She didn't panic. If they found her and she was sacked she wouldn't give a shit. She'd be off to New York next day to a new life. Anyway, she hated this job. Any bit of excitement – like now – was welcome.

Amidst the general scraping back of chairs and the drone of conversation she could make out some of the directors' voices. Then, rising above the rest, she heard Johnson start to speak. She settled down to listen.

Stella had done her best to avoid Steve since the encounter in the street. She still did her mid-morning shopping trips, though. The shops were slack then and she had no time after work. But now she timed her shopping to when she knew he definitely was out. Pam would help her here. She was very good that way. She couldn't say she liked her, but she found her useful and that was all she wanted of anybody. Pam was able to tell her that Steve kept a little black book – which she regularly and secretly inspected – in which he recorded everyone's perceived failings. Stella was in it, she informed her, her recent illegal shopping trip painstakingly recorded.

Stella was suddenly afraid. Why was he keeping information on her? She felt vulnerable and alone. Now Tony's scheme to sabotage the computer began to worry her. What was she being sucked into? What would be management's reaction if they found out?

No matter what happened, she had to keep her job for the sake of her children. That was her sole object in all this, in everything she did. Whatever it took, she would do it.

Mary had received another photo of Sambo. It was similar to the one before, with the cat looking well cared for and positioned in front of a current newspaper headline. With it was a note: LEAVE US IN PEACE OR GET YOUR CAT BACK IN PEACES.

She was terrified now.

She went to Paul and showed it to him. He remembered the chalked outline on the wall. At last he told her of his suspicions.

'Can't you do something?'

'Such as?'

'Can't you go easier on them . . . or whatever they want . . . those awful people?'

'It's a matter of principle.'

'Principle! What about Sambo?'

He looked at her. 'You've changed!'

'What?'

'"Only a bloody cat," you said!'

'Still a helpless dumb creature.'

'You value a cat more than my integrity?'

'Is that what it is?'

'Well . . . do you?'

'Yes.'

'That's nice!'

'Anyway, you seem to have caught integrity like a cold. There was never any mention of it before.'

'Been Mr Nice Guy too long, me.'

'Must have been in somebody else's house, then!'

'You guys are down the tubes. It's official.'

Tony, Paul, Ken and Stella barely acknowledged Pam's breezy forecast of their doom. They'd heard it all before.

'What's new?' snarled Ken.

'Seriously!' she insisted.

'So?' Ken couldn't keep the irritation out of his voice. He resented Pam's easy familiarity, particularly when she was making light of a very serious matter for all of them. She didn't have a wife and two kids and a mortgage to look after. It was easy for the likes of her to make a laugh of everything.

'Heard it from the horse's mouth.'

Then she told how in the boardroom she'd heard the directors decide that, should the architects not prove to be value for money, their work would be subcontracted out to private firms and the in-house technical division, inherited from a more egalitarian era.

'But that's not right!' Ken was genuinely shocked.

'Right's got nothing to do with it,' said Tony. Ken's Boy Scout idea of decent conduct grated with him. It sat uneasily with his support for hanging, whipping and castration – for car thieves.

'Bastards,' said Stella.

Tony felt justified at last in his pronouncements. 'So you see, whatever you do, no matter how hard you work, or how long, or how skilfully, you're up against their agenda. And they'll see to it that they get whatever result they wish. They'll just move the goalposts around.'

Paul was getting angry. He could feel the blood pressure rise. 'So ... what's the point of filling in these time sheets if they're gonna ignore them anyway?'

'I heard the union won't back us if we want to stop them,' said Ken.

'That's right. They won't,' said Tony. 'That's why we only have the one option – the nuclear option – if we want to save our jobs. But no one's to breathe a word of it. Understood?'

All nodded, some more affirmatively than others.

23

Paul's hatred of the brickies grew, and with it his courage. He wouldn't let them intimidate him. And while all the signs pointed to him being a wimpish B, he felt deep down there was an Alpha male just waiting to get out and kick ass.

The weather forecast that morning said frost all day. When he saw the muffled figures busy behind their partly built walls he knew he'd have trouble. Danny was on sick leave, so there was just himself to carry the flag. In frosty weather little is done by the outside trades and he had hoped he wouldn't be faced with any hard decisions today. Now this.

As far as he was concerned, it was freezing and definitely not bricklaying weather. If bricks are laid in frosty weather, the water in the mortar will freeze and the chemical fusion that gives the mortar its strength will not take place. Brick-layers on a morning of low temperatures will stay on in bed, knowing that no money could be made that day. But some days the temperature will hover teasingly around an acceptable level and the men will turn up in the hope that a gradual rise in temperature will allow them to work. Having travelled to site, they are reluctant to go home again with no money earned. So they badger the clerk of works, saying the temperature is rising or the thermometer is wrong – anything to get permission to start laying bricks again.

To end all such discussion, Danny had a large thermometer nailed to the outside of his hut and this was to be the decider. The rule was that if the temperature was at least two degrees and rising, work could commence. Otherwise no work was permitted.

The brickie ganger kept his head down as Paul approached. The peak of the baseball cap was pulled well down over his face like a visor. Try as he might, Paul couldn't get the whirring of a chainsaw out of his head. Around him men were steadily trowelling on the mortar and squeezing bricks into it, bare hands blue with cold.

They had all gone silent. No talking, the only sounds the steady slurp of the trowels slapping on the mortar, and the chundering of the mixer in the background. It was obvious they'd been working all morning. Two feet of fresh brickwork had been added to the blocks.

He hesitated before he spoke. To these men he must seem like an irrelevance, a nuisance in the way of their earning their daily bread. He remembered his window. The phone calls. Sambo. The threats. But a thing had to be done right. He steeled himself, remembering also the fate of Genghis McCann.

Perhaps a casual approach might be best.

'Not think it's a bit cold for bricklaying?'

The brickie didn't break stride. 'Not paid to think. I'm only employed from the neck down.'

'Well, I think it is.' He attempted a bit more gruffness.

The brickie glanced sidewards at him. It was a face that looked as if it had been used for breaking sticks over. And where there should have been eyes, there were two slits through which malevolence glittered out at the world.

'I said it's a bit –'

'Seen worse,' the brickie cut in, not pausing in his work, head still down, avoiding Paul's eyes. His voice was strangely gentle. Kindly almost. The killer eyes when he looked up told a different story.

'Checked the temperature?' said a more confident Paul.

'Oh, God, ay!' The man appeared affronted at the question.

'Surely its below freezing now?'

'Wouldn't say so.'

'Must be.'

The brickie straightened up and looked him in the eye. 'Only one way to find out, then.'

He shouted across to a man working on the block beside Danny's hut. 'Peter, read the thermometer there and shout it out to us!'

Peter, fag in mouth, ambled over to the hut and, leaning on it with his bent arm, brought his face in close, scrutinising the instrument.

Paul wasn't that big an eejit. 'Maybe we should read it together.'

They joined Peter at the hut. Peter, still leaning, kept tapping the thermometer with his fingers to indicate the reading, the fag now transferred from his mouth to between the two yellow-stained digits.

'Look. Four degrees and risin. No bother!'

'OK?' The brickie, cocky now, turned to head back to work.

Paul was puzzled. It was bloody freezing; no doubt about it. But there was the figure and the red column of mercury rising as he watched. Peter kept jabbing at it to emphasise the point.

Then it clicked. Between Peter's attentive fingers his glowing cigarette was angled so that it was almost touching the bottom of the thermometer.

Frig that!

'OK ... It'll all have to come down,' he said. Indignation fired him up.

The men stopped working and looked at him. The brickie ganger leaned forward like he was hard of hearing.

'What's that?'

Paul blinked before the cold steady stare. 'And there's to be no more working till the temperature's right.' He heard his voice too light for the occasion. Nerves.

The brickies looked at each other. Then at their ganger. He regarded Paul in silence for a time. Then he spoke. Quietly.

'You're puttin out our light, fella.'

Danny was back from the sick and on the phone first thing next morning.

'You're not a liked man round here.'

He took it as praise. 'You heard?'

'Did I what!'

'They were warming the thermometer with a cigarette.'

'That old trick!'

'Must think I'm an eejit!'

'Try anythin, those boys.'

'Chancers!'

'Done well to spot it.'

'Sure, you'd do the same.'

Silence.

'Wouldn't you?'

'Those boys?'

'What?'

'Not so sure now.' His voice seemed strained.

'Course you would!'

'Ate their young, those boys.'

Paul laughed. But there'd been no humour in Danny's voice, only a worrying hesitancy.

'Play tig wi' hatchets, those boys.'

Again Paul laughed. There was silence for a moment. Was he playing with him?

'Danny?'

Then, hurriedly, Danny's voice strange, urgent. 'Just this once. What y'say?'

'Say about what?'

'They haven't knocked that brickwork down yet.' Wheedling, apologetic.

He couldn't believe this.

'It's them. They told me to ask.'

'The brickies!'

'Maybe we could let it go . . . this once. What y'think?'

He was pleading! 'You serious, Danny?'

A pause. He heard Danny take a breath.

'Seen that crippled fella?'

'Who?'

'Fella on crutches? Hangs about the entrance?'

'What's that got to do –'

'He wasn't a liked man either.'

Mary was howling on his doorstep. This time he brought her in. He could hardly make sense of what she was saying. She dug into her pocket and thrust another photo at him.

'Look! Poor Sambo!' she wailed.

The photo was as before, with the cat sitting in front of yesterday's newspaper. Apart from the headline, there was one more difference: in this photo Sambo had only one ear.

24

Runian was having a cash-flow problem. To everyone else he was on the pig's back. He'd a huge construction empire, but it was spread over many difficult contracts won with prices that were cut to the bone. In winter such a situation was normal enough, within limits. Bad weather slowed up site works and payments were consequently reduced. But this year was worse than ever. This one big site – over five hundred houses – was to be his saviour. But it was going sick on him. The money just wasn't coming in. His bank was making nervous noises. Suppliers were wary, getting slow in fulfilling orders. These were hard times. Competition for work was tougher than ever. Everybody was working on small margins. If he went under a lot more would go with him: his own employees, subcontractors, suppliers, a sizeable chunk of the council's housing programme. People in high places, no more than he, could afford a collapse.

That bloody architect! A large part of his trouble was down to him. He used to be easy to deal with, but now, whatever'd come over him, he seemed to be going out of his way to find fault with everything. He couldn't let matters stay as they were. As an act of desperation, Maguire and himself made an appointment to meet Johnson, the architect's bossman. Maybe he could make him see sense.

★

A memo from Johnson in a brown envelope through the internal mail was the first Paul knew of his move. He went mad.

Ken looked up from his screen. 'Who's rattled your cage?'

Paul glared at him. 'Don't you know?'

'Know what?'

'Must have told you!'

'Told me what?'

Paul handed him the memo.

'I'm being moved off Runian's job – "for operational reasons".'

'What!'

Ken read the memo.

'First I've heard of this.'

'They haven't told you?'

'Bloody ridiculous!'

'What's goin on?'

'Look . . . they can't do this without consulting me.'

'How'll this look on my personnel file! A troublemaker. It's Runian's behind this.'

Ken was shaking his head. 'This is balls!'

'Bloody right.'

Ken kept looking at it and shaking his head.

His silence worried Paul. 'Will you fight it?'

'I'll . . . I'll . . . yes, of course I'll fight it. They can't do this.'

But apart from initial annoyance, Ken was not that displeased. Lately Paul had become such a thorn in the side of builders that he inflicted stress on anybody connected with his projects, and especially on him as his team leader. He'd heard rumours he had problems at home; maybe that accounted for it. A good architect no doubt, but scrupulousness wasn't a virtue in the hurly-burly of a building site. Maybe a move to a less high-profile job might be better all round.

'Look . . . Leave it with me,' he said.

'They can't just ignore you,' said Paul, hoping to stiffen Ken's resolve. 'Can't just walk over you . . . you, the team leader!'

'No way. I'll hit this on the head.'

'What'll you do?'

'I'll . . .'

'Will you see Johnson?'

'Johnson?'

'Or better still . . . the director?'

'Leave it with me.'

'But what'll you do?'

'I'll . . . I'll . . .'

'What?'

'I'll write a memo.'

That night in the rugby club Paul had a dizzy spell. He and Roy had been sitting together at the time – they had made up, but each knew things could never be quite the same again; the spoken word can never be recalled. Roy reckoned it might have been a bad pint – that twelfth one tasted decidedly odd – but Paul wasn't so sure. The thought that it might be his blood pressure depressed him. Even the prospect of going back to his flat with Claire didn't cheer him up. And then, when she asked him about Mary, his spirits really took a dive. It wasn't that he felt particularly guilty about his infidelity – after all, he was virtually a single man; it was something to do with the comparison between the two.

He felt sad for Mary. She and Claire were both around the same age, but there the similarity ended. Claire still strove to make the best of herself. She was sexy and exciting. Mary had somehow degenerated into a genderless blob, with few interests beyond her teaching job, DIY, and the weekly column she wrote for the *Woodturner's Weekly*. When they married at twenty-five she was a beauty. But what hurt most was that she didn't seem to care. When he would try delicately to point out her failings, her constant retort was, 'You're no oil painting yourself.'

Back in the flat came the flaccid evidence that the tablets were kicking in – or so he told the disappointed Claire. But he wasn't sure if it was true or not. Their routine grapplings were beginning to pall with him. And he knew she sensed it.

She wasn't inclined to be understanding. 'You'd better get yourself seen too,' she said as she dressed. She was annoyed. Earlier in the evening she'd turned down an offer from a man ten years younger than Paul. If she hurried she could get back before last orders. He might still be there.

'Sorry,' he said.

'Don't mention it,' she said icily.

As she swept out of the room, he knew she'd never be back.

She turned briefly in the doorway. 'By the way, I thought you'd better know – I faked everything. I've had more fun with the corner of my spin-dryer than I ever had with you!'

Romeo and Juliet, eat your hearts out!

Ken's wishy-washy response annoyed Paul: a memo! He went straight to Tony, who informed the union. It wasn't on. Management moving people about at the behest of a builder! It was Paul now, but it could be any of them next. A few days later, to his and everybody's surprise, a memo arrived from Johnson saying the move had been cancelled. Evidently the union still had some clout.

The more Paul thought about it, the more angry he got. Attacking his professional reputation – and all because he was trying to do his job properly! Right, gloves-off time! He determined to be even more strict on site. If the builder wanted to play rough – for it must have been Runian who complained – well, he could play rough too. But he had a problem: he needed Danny as a back-up. And he just wasn't. Asking for those walls not to be demolished, knowing well that they were built in the frost, was a bad sign. This wasn't Danny the scourge of the brickies. Danny had changed.

On the first site visit after his move had been recinded, he had his feeling confirmed. In fact, everything on site seemed to have changed; nothing was quite as it had been. Danny seemed more distant, the brickies even more hostile. Runian and Maguire just passed themselves with the barest of civilities. But it was Danny who worried him most. Danny, his anchor, his main man. Danny, his eyes and ears on the site when he wasn't there. Danny, on whose experience and judgement he placed such store, was now to all intents and purposes a zombie. His former monosyllabic responses seemed positively garrulous compared to now.

'You OK, Danny?'

He had come into the clerk of works hut and found Danny sitting looking pale and withdrawn, staring out of the window. He appeared not to hear him. The brickie ganger was just leaving as Paul entered. He slunk out, squeezing past him in the doorway, eyes averted, with never a word or even a grunt of acknowledgement.

'You two have a row or what?' he enquired after the brickie was out of hearing.

Silence.

'Danny . . .'

'I heard.'

The clipped reply shocked him.

'What's up?'

'Nothin.'

'Come on . . . There's something!'

'You don't want to know.'

'Danny . . .'

'You don't want to know, I said!'

Paul was taken aback. 'Suit yourself.'

The monthly site meeting that followed in the builder's hut took on an unaccustomed formal aspect. The state of the job was discussed, but the old easy exchanges, the banter, the racy anecdotes were missing. As he left to go, he turned to Danny to make a final effort at tackling whatever it was between them, but Danny had pointedly turned back to staring at the window.

Outside a sudden wind blew up a dust storm, skittering a hail of dried mud, sand and brick dust across the site. An empty tin of cat food frolicked amidst the rubble. He drove out through the site gates, peering through the blizzard of dust – and almost colliding with the man on crutches, who was directly in his path. He stood on his brakes. His foot travelled to the floor. Nothing. He pumped the pedal. Nothing. He pumped again. He pumped and pumped. The car came to a stop.

The man on crutches hobbled round the bonnet.

'I seen them!'

Paul was too shocked to take in what was said.

'Seen them under your car. Look!'

The man beckoned. Paul got out.

At the rear of the car, the man waved a crutch at the ground. A glistening trail led from the site to where the car now rested. He got on his knees and peered under the car. He saw the last few drops of brake fluid drip from the severed pipe.

When he looked up the man had gone.

It was when he got home that he noticed that his jacket, which he'd left in the car, was missing, and along with it his wallet and credit cards, his rugby club membership card, etc.

Two days later the clubhouse was burnt to the ground.

25

Pam completed the jigsaw.

'Dynamite!' She was phoning from somewhere in the building. In the background the sound of a shower hissed invitingly and sinfully – it was ten thirty in the morning. 'Be down in a minute. Tell you all then.'

She came in, gleaming, freshly shampooed, with a faint whiff of vodka about her, and alight with her news. Tony and Paul were waiting. Tony guessed that what she had to say was not for general broadcasting; her news was always of the purest gold. He didn't tell Ken or any of the others. Broken reeds, they were. He'd come to the conclusion that whatever battles had to be fought he couldn't depend on them. Paul was pleased to be one of the elect.

'Wait t'you hear ...' She rushed into the story. 'Me and my friend were parked out at Shaw's bridge – y'know, the big car park down by the river.'

'Condom alley,' said Tony.

'You've been there?'

Tony blushed. 'Not since my single days.'

'Hey ... Never told us you had a boyfriend!' Paul was slightly peeved. Good job he'd never made a move there.

'Oh, nothing serious. I just use him for sexual gratification. Anyway, as I was saying ... It's about one in the morning and the place is filling up with cars – the usual. There's no lights anywhere . . .'

'Maybe Paul here's too young to hear this?'

'Listen. Two cars came in together beside us and turned off their lights, but not before the lights of one had picked out the registration number of the other.'

She paused, her eyes brimming with the goodies she was about to deliver.

'Well?' said Tony.

'Guess whose car it was?' She looked from Tony to Paul.

'Whose?'

'Give up?'

'Frig's sake, Pam . . . !'

'Johnson, our revered boss!' She sat back, looking from one to the other.

They were shocked. Johnson was such a dry stick, they would never have associated him with midnight car parks.

'Sly dog,' said Paul, appreciatively.

'Suppose the man's entitled to a private life like the rest of us,' said Tony.

'Depends on the private life.' She was enjoying this.

'So?'

'You haven't asked who was in the other car.'

'Look, I don't care.' Tony affected indifference.

'I do,' said Paul. Johnson and he were of an age. It was interesting to compare notes. He hated to think of him getting more than himself.

'That's the really meaty bit.'

'Gossips, that's what you two are,' said Tony casually, riveted.

'Just glimpsed his face as he got into Johnson's car . . .'

Tony sat upright.

'Fuck!'

'A man!' said Paul.

'Yes.'

'Jesus!' Paul was shocked. This sort of thing brought down the Roman Empire. What would it do to the council's architects' department!

'And a very well-known man.'

'Who?' Paul's eyes bulged.

'Certain it was him. Seen his picture from the TV and papers and stuff . . .'

'Who?'

'Ah, you're interested now, all right!'

'Johnson!' Paul was still taking it in.

'Pam, for Christ's sake!'

'Y'ready?'

'Yes.'

Her eyes gleamed with revelations as she looked from one eager face to the other.

'Frank Moriarty!'

'Wha . . .'

'I'm certain.'

Tony stared at her, then turned and gave a quick look round the office. He leaned closer, dropping his voice.

'*The* Frank Moriarty?'

'I'm sure.'

'You're jokin,' said Paul. 'Frank "Legs" Moriarty?'

Moriarty, who was no dancer, had acquired his sobriquet not for anything to do with his own anatomy, but rather for the attention he paid to other people's. It was chiefly as a leg breaker that he had made his name during his juvenile delinquent phase of petty crime. But since then he had discovered patriotism paid better and had moved on to more terminal preoccupations, though it was said that he still liked to keep his hand in with a bit of legwork when the mood took him. His day job was that of an entrepreneur with a finger in a lot of pies, and a hand round a lot of throats. He was a very serious man. Chiefly he was known as a supplier of subcontract labour squads to builders. In a city carved up between various political and sectarian factions, only certain people could be employed in certain areas – horses for courses. No builder in his part of the city could operate without his approval, and consequently without his workers. He guaranteed a supply of labour for the contractors; they in turn would pay him a fee and would employ his security firm. On top of this, the workers would contribute a percentage of their wages to party funds, his party funds: the Frank Moriarty Republican Party.

'Johnson and him! Jesus!' said Tony. 'It was bad enough hearing about Rock Hudson!'

'Arse bandits!' Paul too was shocked.

'Stupid! It's nothin to do with that ... unless they're into orgies,' said Pam. 'Three other guys got into Johnson's car as well.'

'Three? But ...'

'It was a meeting, y'eejits. A secret meeting.'

'A meeting ...' Tony checked around the room.

'Dodgy, ay?' said Pam.

'I'll say,' said Tony. 'Hardly the sort of company you imagine our boss to be keeping, particularly when you know who Moriarty's brother-in-law is.'

'Who?' said Paul.

'Who!'

'Who?' insisted Paul.

'Thought you knew. One of the council's biggest building contractors?' said Tony.

'Christ's sake, who?'

'It's your man, Runian!'

Paul went cold.

'Common knowledge that.'

Paul didn't speak. Wasn't common knowledge to him.

Runian and Frank Moriarty!

'They hate each other, mind,' said Tony. 'But still.'

It was all starting to come together: Runian, Johnson and now Moriarty. Now there was the link between the brickies and his personnel files.

Other things started to come together too. He thought of his cut brake fluid pipe, the scratches on his car, the phone calls. Sambo. He'd put it all down to mindless vandalism. He had tried to diminish its importance; it was less scary that way.

That option wasn't there any more.

26

The morning Sambo's ear arrived in the post Mary called in the police.

'Seen you before, haven't we, sir,' said the policeman, fixing Paul with a stare reserved for mass murderers.

'He's my . . . husband. Remember?' Mary's irritated tone attempted to warn him off pursuing any domestic issues. To no avail.

'Separated, as I remember?'

'Yes . . . separated.'

'Just so as we know what's what.'

The four of them, Paul, Mary and the two policemen, stood around the coffee table. They looked down at the piece of kitchen towel which contained the bloodied membrane.

They were all silent for a moment.

'Well?'

'Well what exactly, madam?'

'What steps have you taken to find our cat?'

The policemen smiled at each other.

'It *is* a cat, madam,' said one.

'I know what it is,' she snapped.

'I mean, no offence, madam, but it's not exactly Arkle that's missing.'

'Just a matter of scale!' she fought back.

He wouldn't be beaten. 'True, madam, but it's easier to find a horse in a haystack than a cat.' He chortled quietly at what he considered his debating coup.

Paul controlled his anger. The fat one looked like a big shoot-to-kill fan. Definitely a case for bottling it up.

Mary appealed to his gentler nature. 'But his poor ear! And these photos! What's going on?'

Thumbs tucked firmly inside their flak jackets, the policemen pondered Sambo's ear.

'Any problem with neighbours?'

'No.'

Bigmouth knew Paul was fond of the cat. Would he do it out of spite? No. Dickhead as he was, he wouldn't be cruel. Mary herself in a fit of rage, seeing the cat as a smaller, hairier version of her husband? He dismissed the thought.

The policemen turned to Paul.

'Like cats, do you, sir?'

Here we go again. It was obvious he was their main suspect. The estranged husband – it's always him. He began to panic.

'Me? I liked Sambo. I loved him.' He felt ridiculous declaring his love for a cat. But these were desperate times.

'I'm a dog man myself,' said the thin one. 'Can't see the point of cats. But I wouldn't be cruel.' He picked up the photo. He mellowed. 'Look at 'im! Looks like he's sittin there listening to us.'

'Half listening,' corrected the other.

They tittered.

Paul felt the drumming in his veins. 'So what happens now?'

'Like I said, sir, it *is* a cat.'

'We've established that. Nothing, that what you mean?'

'We'll await developments.'

And they left.

★

Management knew there was something not right. Inexplicably, the architects' production figures were suddenly soaring. The computer department fine-checked them, but nothing was found. And now Johnson was querying them. Steve knew it would be quite a coup if he could solve the mystery and he had a hunch the answer lay with the architects themselves. So the moment he saw Stella's guilty face staring at him from the crowd at the hole-in-the-wall machine, he knew what he had to do.

'Good morning, Stella!' he said, once again looking meaningfully at his watch.

As before, he was on his own legitimate errand when he met her. She nodded and scuttled away. Game, set and match! He was about to make his first citizen's arrest.

Some hours later he sat across his desk from her, arms folded.

'You know what I want to talk to you about, don't you?'

He had let her stew all afternoon. He knew she'd be hoping against hope not to hear from him; that he'd let this transgression pass, as he had the other. He liked to think of her wondering, fretting. Then, after a suitable interval, when she fancied he would indeed have forgotten, when she would be relaxing with the thought that she was safe, he struck.

'No,' she said in a weak voice.

She had come up the moment he phoned. As she entered the room he made a point of walking past and closing the door behind her. Wordlessly, he took his seat behind his desk and motioned her into hers.

'There's no point in me reading out the relevant clause in the conditions of service, Stella, is there?'

She said nothing. Just stared at him. A rabbit caught in the headlights.

'We have to talk, Stella.'

He saw her hands shake. He was beginning to enjoy this.

He would show her who was what around here.

'Absence from your work station without just cause is a sackable offence. You do realise that, don't you?'

She went white. He knew what words had effect.

'Although it's not my immediate responsibility, as a manager I can't ignore it. It's a very serious matter.'

Already she was close to tears. This was going to be easy.

'I . . . I . . .' she began. Then stopped.

'Well?'

She said nothing.

'Twice I've caught you red-handed. Right? What am I expected to do? I'm a manager. I have responsibilities.'

'Steve, look . . . I only nipped out for a minute . . . that's all.'

'Once maybe . . . But twice!'

'Just for a minute . . . that's all!'

'You see my position, don't you? What am I supposed to do? I'm duty bound to tell the personnel people.'

'It won't happen again. I promise.'

'It's stealing public money, y'know. You're being paid for time you haven't worked.'

Her head hung down. She said nothing.

Now was the time. 'There's maybe . . . one way we might overlook this,' he began.

She looked up.

'You could do the council a favour.'

'What do you mean?'

He leaned forward, his face close to hers. 'There's something going on with the production figures, but none of us know what it is. We know there's fiddling somewhere, but we can't see where.'

He paused and leaned back into his chair. 'You want to talk about it?'

Paul didn't like lying to Pam. Even a bit of a white lie. She was very straight. She looked you in the eye and said what she thought, and expected to be replied to in kind.

He was to take her out to site with him again today. She'd been looking forward to it; the arrangements were made. Then the phone rang.

'Paul? Joan here.'

His heart jumped. He hadn't heard from her for ages. Then his spirits dropped. Was it the return of the shite monster?

'Paul, I've got a problem . . .'

So it was the shite monster.

'I've got one of my Housing Institute exams next week . . .'

No shite monster yet.

'. . . and I was wondering if you could help me with some building construction revision I'm doing. Would you mind?'

Is the Pope a catholic!

'No problem, Joan.'

'Really? That's great. Maybe lunch together. Something like that. You could go over a few questions with me.'

'Sure.'

'You're awfully good, Paul.'

His heart pounded. Could this be doing him damage? Physical damage. He thought of the medical diagram of the human body he'd seen in the doctor's room, the myriad threadlike veins carrying the blood to wherever it was needed most. Could this excitement be drawing it all to his heart? He knew of a tall, thin friend who had an enormous penis and every time he had an erection he fainted as the blood drained from his upper body. His mind filled with an image of millions of arteries dilating before this torrent of blood. He felt weak.

'Look, I'm free this lunch hour . . .'

Ah, no!

'Today?'

'Oh, is today a problem?'

Pam . . . the friggin site visit!

'Well . . .'

He saw Joan as a fish on the end of his line and he was trying to reel her in. One slip and she could be off and away.

'No. No, that's fine. Where?'

In the dim light of the snug she looked more beautiful than ever. The two gins he'd had made him even more appreciative. They also made him more talkative. He told her all about his life, his loves, his plans, Mary, the separation. He told her everything. He saw their reflections in the wall mirror opposite. They looked a handsome couple together. He didn't look old. He looked just right for her.

'Y'know, you're wasted there,' she said in a rare gap in his flow.

'Where?'

'Oh, I'm sure you're a great architect, Paul. You obviously love your work. But, and I hope you don't mind me saying this, it's a bit limiting, isn't it?'

'What way?'

'I mean, you deal with little patches of development, like an estate here, a few dozen houses there . . . that sort of thing.'

'I enjoy that. Each job's a new challenge.'

'Yes, but . . . there's a bigger picture . . . like . . . like strategic planning for a whole city. Your imagination and creativity would be much more recognised in that field, don't you think?'

He was flattered. Was she right? He'd often felt himself undervalued.

'But where?'

'So happens that we're getting into that whole field: town planning, all that.'

'Housing management?'

'Yes. Why not? We know the housing need. How big it is, where it is. It's a small step from that to strategic planning, isn't it?'

'Well, yes. But . . .'

'Of course, we wouldn't have the creativity, the technical background . . . That's where we'd need an architectural resource . . .' She leaned forward and laid her hand on his arm. 'That's where you could come into your own, Paul.'

'Me?'

Beneath the table her knees nudged against his. He felt faint. He loved this intimacy, the closeness; listening to her voice, his face bathing in her scent. But being thought of as a resource brought him down to earth somewhat. A bag of coal was a resource; he considered himself, and all architects, as the fire. But such discussion was for another time. It was the here and now that mattered.

She put one slender, exquisitely manicured finger to her lips, then looked swiftly around the room before bringing those huge blue eyes to bear on him again. 'Look, you're not to say, but we need someone right now.'

Her conspiratorial tone drew him closer. 'Y'mean . . . like an architectural adviser?' he said huskily.

'That sort of thing. I hear it'd be a grade above yours. A promotion. More money. More status. Would you be interested?'

So much was happening so fast. And the gin was making it all unreal.

'I'd think about it, sure.'

Joan looked at her watch. Then quickly flicked through her Filofax.

'God, I better move. I've a meetin at two.'

He started to rise. She pushed out a restraining hand and

flashed him a big smile. 'No, you take it easy. Finish your drink. Look, we'll be in touch. Bye!'

And she was gone.

He sat back, relaxing into his third gin. Only when he had it finished did it dawn on him that she hadn't asked one question about building construction.

'Why did you lie?'

The office was quiet. Paul had spent the afternoon in a gin-induced torpor. Drinking during the day meant death to production. He sat clicking lines onto his screen, but to little effect. Ken had given him a few funny looks, but it was after five now and he'd gone home. Most people had gone home. He was too busy mentally stripping Joan to hurry anywhere.

Pam had appeared at his side.

'Why?' she repeated. 'No point in denying it. I saw you and her going into the pub.'

He felt like a rat.

Her stare pierced him. 'Y'know, I really don't find your love life all that fascinating. I just like to be told the truth.'

'Pam, listen . . .'

She flounced off. As she reached the door to the back stairs, she turned. There was a hint of tears in her eyes.

'Know where I've been this last hour?'

'Pam . . .'

'Do you even bloody well care?'

Suddenly he was sober. Something had happened. This was a different Pam. He sat up.

'Consoling my friend up in the computer room . . . that's where,' she said.

'What?'

'For you friggin lot!'

'What? What about?'

'What y'think?'

'I've no idea.'

'Does the extra nought mean anything to you?'

His heart stopped. 'Oh.'

'Exactly. Somehow Steve's rumbled it.'

'But how?'

'I don't know. My friend had to say it was just her own stupid mistake. Had to crawl. What the frig else?'

'Och, Pam . . .'

'Oh, she doesn't give a damn about the bloody job, but they gave her a right bollocking. And I got her into all that!'

'Look . . .'

'She's been threatened with the sack, the police – you name it. And all over you, who can't even tell the truth. I'm sorry I fuckin bothered!'

'Pam . . .'

But she was off, crashing the door behind her.

Funny how jealousy affects people.

Tony was alarmed. But Pam's friend had stuck by her story and management had to accept it. However, the end result was that they would all have to take on an extra job each to make their monthly production targets. It was that or show big losses and possible close-down – and outside employment prospects were bleak. Tony said it was impossible, given the workload everybody had on. He, Tony, would continue at his own pace. It was up to others to do what they thought right.

Ken spread the printout on Paul's desk.

'No way!' said Paul.

'There's the figures,' said Ken.

'I can't take on another site!'

'The figures say different.'

'You know they're rubbish.'

'The directors believe them. That's what counts, Paul.'

'Even if they're rubbish?'

Ken was getting irritated. 'Look, Paul, we're bloody stuck with them.'

'But Runian's site is more time and trouble than any three sites put together! You know that!'

Ken pulled a face. 'Taking far too much of your time, that site.'

Paul sensed a rebuke. 'Oh?'

'Well, it is.'

'No more than it needs.'

Ken tapped the sheet with his biro. 'You'll just have to take this job, Paul.'

'But Runian's – '

'Frig Runian's! Look, Paul, I'm telling you ... You'll have to take it.'

The bastard was trying to bully him! He felt the arteries dilating. The surge of blood swishing through the capillaries. The pumping, pumping. Professional pride was at stake here. He sat up straight.

'I'll not take on more work than I can be professionally responsible for.'

Ken laughed. 'Aw, come off it, Paul!'

'Off what?'

'This high-horse stuff.'

Paul felt his temper rising. 'It's called being professional.'

'We've all got to do what has to be done.'

'What's that mean?'

'Look ... we're all just employees here. We do what we're told by who pays our wages.'

'Up to a point.'

'What?'

That was the moment he felt the call. 'We're more than employees.'

Ken looked at him. 'Come again?'

He felt the spirit descend onto him. He knew the others were listening. He was Martin Luther King in Alabama, Nelson Mandela, Che Guevara, Moses leading the Israelites through the Red Sea. To him had fallen the honour of raising the banner of professional integrity. Somewhere far off an orchestra welled up.

'We've a wider duty: a duty to society, to truth, to beauty . . .'

'What?' Ken gawped.

'We aren't nine-to-five clock-watchers. We are artists, shapers of the environment, moulders of civic taste, cultural barometers. We are a special breed. We are a creative élite. We are *Architects*!'

Ken stared in amazement.

'Bollocks!' he said, and stormed off.

Paul was glad he'd let it all out. He felt better. He felt liberated.

'Excellent!' Tony was beaming. He smacked him on the back. 'That was giving it to him, mate!' he said.

But he was the only one. Other than Val, that is, who thought it was very brave but hoped there wouldn't be any trouble.

Stella was concerned. 'Well, quite honestly I think Paul's flipped his lid,' she said. 'Face it, Tony, we've no choice in this.'

'So we let ourselves be dictated to by accountants!' He looked around the glum faces.

'It's what it boils down to,' said Paul in support.

'Maybe it's all right for you, but some of us can't risk losing our jobs,' said Stella. 'I certainly can't.'

'So we let them walk all over us? What about pride?'

'Can't afford pride.'

Tony was about to launch into an attack, when he hesitated. He too had a mortgage, a wife, three kids, a car. What would he do without his job? Could he afford pride? He dismissed the treacherous thought.

'Well, I'm with Paul. And that's that!'

27

Maguire was back from a short holiday. Tanned and relaxed-looking, he brought an exotic touch to the shabby site hut. He dusted the timber bench with his handkerchief before sitting down. The usual site meeting attenders were there: Runian, his foreman, Danny and Paul.

Maguire surveyed them all. 'Great to be back to happy smiling faces again.'

They glowered back at him.

He held out his arms defensively. 'Only a joke. Only a joke.'

'Let's get on with it!' barked Runian.

Paul went through the various routine items. But after a while Danny said he wasn't feeling well and was going outside for some air.

He definitely wasn't himself.

Afterwards, outside the hut, Danny excused himself from their usual site inspection walk-about. He still wasn't feeling well. He said he was going home. Paul went on alone, convinced now that Danny's health was the reason for his strangeness lately.

He passed the group of plasterers out having a tea break in the weak winter sun. They were working on a previous more advanced stage of the development. A happy-go-lucky bunch they were, countrymen perched amid the rubble and debris of construction. They sat outside the doorway of the house they were plastering, with the choking plaster dust ghosting out from the blackness behind.

'Grand day!' one said.

He nodded back. Didn't do to get too familiar.

'Fella askin after you the other day,' another said. 'Wanted to know which was the archeeteck's car.'

Paul stopped.

'Me?'

'The archeeteck. That's what he said. Right, boys?'

'Know who it was?' He tried not to sound too interested.

'Said his name was Catney. Tom Catney.'

'From round here, is he?'

'Wouldn't know him from a crow.'

'What was he like?'

'A great big hoor of a man. Maybe six six.'

Paul knew nobody like that. He felt uneasy.

'An' that was only 'is arm,' said another.

'Oh, a great hoor of a man surely.'

'Big scar down his cheek.'

They saw his unease. They decided to enjoy it.

'He'd be the type you wouldn't want to meet on a dark night.'

'Sorta fella would strip a hen roost and no bother to him.'

'You'd rather lend him than owe him, that sort of a fella.'

As he walked on he heard them laugh among themselves. Were they having him on? Their idea of a joke? But then, his car. He hurried out of the site.

As he reached his car, he bent down and checked under it – the memory of his brake fluid pipe was still with him.

'You're learnin.'

He didn't hear the man approach. He straightened up quickly.

The man with the crutch was standing over him. 'They're watchin you, y'know.'

'What?'

'Remember the last time? A warnin, that was!'

'What are you on about?'

'I'm just tellin you. You're causin them grief. They don't like that, that parcel o' hoors!'

'Look . . . I don't know what you're talkin about.'

The man flourished his crutch. 'See me! They did this. I'll never work again, see!'

Paul got the key in the lock, preparing for a quick getaway. The man followed him round to the driver's door.

'Y'know what I did to get this? A few sheets of plaster-board! I took a few friggin sheets of plasterboard and they broke my legs. Should'a been just one leg. Can't even trust them to break yer legs proper. There's rules, y'know! An' they gimme a whole pile o'money for the taxi. So I thought. What was it? Eyetalian – worth about ten fuckin p! Parcel o'hoors!'

As he accelerated away, the man was still shouting.

'A few sheets of friggin plasterboard! Y'hear me! That's nothin to what they're gettin away with. Nothin! I could tell you things . . .'

In his rear-view mirror he saw a group of men emerge from within the site and point in the man's direction. The man scuttled away.

When he got back to the office there was a note to ring Joan.

The thrill of anticipation, he got it every time. He cleared his throat, even combed his hair before calling back.

'Thanks for returning my call so quickly, Paul . . .'

Maybe he shouldn't be quite so eager. Might frighten her off.

'That matter we discussed, it's definite.'

What was she talking about? Then he remembered: the job.

'Look, can we meet?' she said.

He tried to control his eagerness. 'Sure, I'll be free on . . .'

'Today, if possible.'

Holy God, she sounded as keen as himself!

'Sure. Will I come down to you?'

She paused. 'No. Be better if we meet outside the office. More private. Same place as last time? I'll see you inside.'

Before leaving the office, he looked around. Why he should worry about Pam seeing him he just wasn't sure. She'd been cool with him ever since the last time. Jealous as hell. Pity about her, really. In fact, that morning was the first time she'd spoken to him civilly in a week.

'You've forgotten to clock in, fuck face,' she'd said.

It was an improvement on silence.

'Three thousand extra a year.'

Joan smiled across the table. She threw back her head, exhaled a great gust of smoke and daintly flicked ash into the tray.

'Well?'

Paul couldn't take his eyes off her.

'What do you think?'

He wasn't thinking. Just looking.

'Paul?'

'Oh, yeah. Sounds good.'

'Interested, then?'

He pulled himself together. He cleared his throat. 'Ah . . . is it definite?'

'Bounced the idea off Brian . . . er . . . Mr Johnson. "Brilliant," he said. "No problem." Well?'

But Paul was only half listening. The job was all Joan

seemed to want to talk about. In fact he'd completely forgotten about it after their first meeting. To tell the truth, he wasn't really interested. He was an architect; he'd no ambition to be a desk-bound administrator. He was flattered she thought of him – there must be some spark there. He decided not to disillusion her just yet.

'Ah . . . sounds great, Joan.'

'Good! Look, I'll get you more gen on it soon.'

Now was the time to strike.

'Joan?'

'Yes?'

'I was wondering . . .' He paused.

For a moment he caught what seemed to be a hint of panic in her eyes. Then, suddenly standing up, she consulted her watch and snatched her Filofax all in one movement. She laughed.

'God, Paul . . . What must you think of me! Here I am rushing off again. I've calls to make and I should be at my first one in ten minutes!'

He stood up. 'Joan?'

'I'll be in touch,' she interrupted. She gave a cheery wave as she went out of the door.

The moment had passed.

Ken got a bollocking from Johnson, who got a bollocking from the directors, who got a bollocking from the council manager, who got a bollocking from local politicians over delays on Runian's site. As Paul's team leader, Ken now had to write to the directors explaining the situation.

'Landed me in it, this has,' he grumbled. It was obvious the remark was directed at Paul.

Paul felt his hackles rise. 'A lousy builder. What do they expect!'

'No matter. Doesn't look very professional, all these

delays, now does it?'

He felt the drumming, the arteries dilating. Something had to give.

'Could be worse . . .'

Ken looked up. 'Pardon?'

No pulling back now. Pressure release valve full open! Let it go!

'One of us could have had an extension built free by one of our builders . . .'

A tic below Ken's left eye started jumping.

'Now that's what I call unprofessional!' said Paul.

28

Steve caught Stella's eye as she hurried through the entrance lobby.

He smiled.

She shivered. She was in his power and he lost no chance of reminding her of it. No words were needed; just took a look to remind her who was in charge. It constituted a secret intimacy between them – reluctantly so on her part. She hated him. She hated herself. She was an informer. A traitor. She was everything everybody decent abhorred. She thought of Tony's reproving stares should he ever know. And the others. None of them really liked her anyway. They must never know. She had made Steve promise not to tell Johnson that they were all in on it. The story was to be that he had stumbled on the extra nought by dint of his own detective work; that it was all just a careless mistake. This version suited him; it made him look vigilant, on the ball. Then she thought of her children. She needed her job. Whatever it took, her first loyalty was to her family. Nothing else mattered.

'What's this with you and Steve?' Pam appeared from nowhere, standing over her, hands on hips.

She jumped. 'What?'

'The other day. You were in with him for ages. Rumour has it you're having an affair!'

'What!'

'Only a joke! Only a joke!' She laughed. 'I mean, how could anybody! He's so friggin ugly! I bet when he was born the midwife didn't know what end to smack. Must be the world's most ineligible bachelor – he's an Olympic contender!'

Stella relaxed. 'Oh . . . he was talking about this market-testing rubbish. Don't know why he picks on me.'

'Thought he might've had you in about your shopping spree the other day.'

'Me! No!'

'Sort of thing the wee rat enjoys. None of his business either. Just likes to appear the big man, so he does.'

'Well, it wasn't that.'

'Tony's the one I'd worry about,' said Pam. 'Suits himself when he comes and goes. Only a matter of time before Steve notices it.'

Stella was relieved that the spotlight was off her. She still felt bad. But what she'd done, she'd done for her children. Whatever it took, she wouldn't put her job at risk. Nothing mattered more than that.

Danny delivered a bombshell: a sick line for two months! Nervous disability, it said. Paul felt confirmed in all his suspicions about the man's health. The council was trying to get another clerk of works to cover, but in the meantime Paul was on his own.

He got the foreman to walk round with him on his site inspection.

'You'll be visitin him?' said the foreman.

'Danny?'

'Just thought you might be visitin him.'

It hadn't occurred to him. They didn't have that relationship. Always at a distance, Danny. But still, be a friendly thing to do. He realised he'd no idea where Danny lived. They'd have his address in the office. He'd drop out some time.

The foreman laughed. 'Might get a surprise there.'

'What?'

'Oh, you'll see.'

Before he could enquire further, he was distracted by a commotion at the entrance gate. He turned just in time to see a crowd of men, in the middle of whom was the man on crutches being hustled away. He was shouting as he went. Paul couldn't make out what he was saying above the noise of the machinery. The plasterers were ghost-white with plaster dust as they stood at their dark entrances and looked out on the madness of Belfast.

The foreman turned as well. 'Fuckin headcase!' he said.

'A brickie, wasn't he?'

'Fucker was stealin stuff off the site. Security caught him.'

'What happened to him?'

The foreman smirked. 'Caught his legs in a mangle or somethin.'

'What?'

'Pity it wasn't his head.'

Paul stared after the scrum of workmen.

'Friggin nuisance, that's what he is.'

Paul kept looking after the retreating figures. They had now ejected the man and were coming back into the site. The man made angry gestures with his crutch.

'Is he safe?'

'There's a wee want there if you ask me!'

'Jumped out at me a few times.'

'You don't want to heed him,' said the foreman. 'Head's gone. Says anythin, that fella.'

The foreman started to lead him round the site, but Paul suspected he'd be taking him to places where there were no problems. He insisted he'd go where he wanted to go, and in the end handed the foreman a long list of items of bad workmanship that needed remedying.

The foreman looked glum. 'Gettin as bad as Danny, you are,' he said. And, as he turned away, 'An' look what happened to him!'

Paul stared at him.

The foreman laughed. 'Only jokin,' he said.

It was about then Paul started getting phone calls in his flat – and the first word of Sambo. How did they know his new number? He hadn't given it to personnel, so there was nothing on his file. Only Danny had it, in case of emergencies. He would get them at two or three in the morning.

'Listenyoufuckinbastard . . . Get off our backs or you'll keep gettin yer cat back – in instalments. We're sendin them to your wife so's she can sew them all together again.'

Next day Mary got another ear in the post.

Then there'd be other calls, cursing and threatening what would be done to him if he didn't get off the site. It all fell into place now: Sambo, the cat chalked on the wall, Tom Catney. Maybe even the fire at the club! He would come into work bleary-eyed and fit for nothing. He'd mentioned it to Ken. Ken just shrugged, said he should tell the police, but anyway they'd probably enough on their plate without disgruntled workers. Ken advised him to avoid the site for a bit, stay in the office more. But he'd get the calls there too. One day Tony, passing, picked up Paul's phone. He listened for a bit before Paul came over, then slammed it down.

Paul saw the shock on his face. 'Get an earful, did you?'

'Jesus . . . whose cage have you rattled?'

Paul shrugged.

'How long's this been goin on?'

Paul told him.

'Of course, you know where it's coming from?' By this stage the whole office knew of his difficulties.

'Runian's site, I suppose.'

'Seems you're doing your job too well for some people.'

'I hope so!'

'You don't have to take this, y'know. Just say the word . . . A move to another site maybe . . . The union would back you.'

It was the easy way out. But he'd finished taking the easy way. No more bottling things up. 'That's just what they want.'

Tony beamed at him. 'That's the stuff! And remember, the union's behind you all the way. All the way.'

Not very reassuring. To Paul, the union fulfilled the function of the ropes around a boxing ring: they didn't stop you getting hit, they just kept you in the game.

A short time later Pam came down with the latest production reports.

'Nudes in them this week, boys!'

Paul felt his being whammed against the back of his head. It was like old times. The rift was over.

The office car park to the rear of the building was ill lit at the best of times, but since vandals had knocked out half the streetlights it was hard to locate your car. Paul felt his way along the aisles of cars and as he reached his own a shuffling tapping sound made him turn round.

'Hey, archeeteck!'

The headcase! Man and crutch were silhouetted against what light remained.

'Hey!'

He'd just got into the car when the man thrust something paper at him through his rapidly closing door. As he roared out onto the open road, he scattered a few men standing at the car-park entrance. He hadn't seen them there when he came in. Out of the corner of his eye, he was aware of them turning and racing after the fast-disappearing figure of the cripple.

When he got back to the flat he looked at the piece of paper. It was a torn fragment of his own site drawing. Scrawled on it was a note, 'Look here,' and an X marked on a corner of a house, like a child's treasure map.

He threw it away.

'You understand this is as embarrassing for me as it is for you,' said Steve in a very unembarrassed voice.

This was the second time in a week he had someone sitting across the desk from him, someone who didn't want to be there; someone who knew he, Steve, for once had the whip hand. It felt good. He could get to like this.

He pushed across the table the paper with the notes of when Tony had been out of the office without permission.

'Explain!' he said.

It was the 'Explain!' that did it. Up until six months before, Steve had worked alongside him and had distinguished himself by his outstanding mediocrity. Now he was the poacher turned gamekeeper, for then there had been no greater skiver than he. For ten minutes Tony had had to listen to him crowing about how many people he had caught out skiving off and how that could undermine the new market-testing exercise.

Tony had had enough. He fixed Steve with a steely glare.

'Look ... I'm not paid by the bloody hour. I'm a creative person, a professional. Whether I work ten hours or a hundred hours a week is irrelevant. It's what I do, what I produce in bricks and mortar on time and within budget, that's the only true measurement of my worth.'

He stood up and leaned across the table, waving Steve's paper under his nose.

'See this, Steve?'

Steve shrank from the glint in his eye.

'Stick it!'

He left the room.

Danny lived on the northern outskirts of the city, where the red-brick tide ran up against the rising ground of the hills. Here suburban streets backed on to fields and open country-side. It wasn't a part of the town Paul was familiar with and the looming bulk of the hill came as a surprise – but not such a surprise as Danny's house itself. It dominated the end of a tree-lined cul-de-sac, a double-fronted pre-war villa with extensive gardens front and rear. Children played on a swing in the front garden. As he walked up the drive, he noticed a partly finished extension to the rear – an extension which looked like it would double the size of the original house. It was built in the same bricks that were being used on Runian's site.

He started to get a funny feeling.

The children ran over to him.

'Your daddy in?' he asked.

'He's out workin, mister,' said a miniature version of Danny.

'Working?'

A woman hurried out the front door. 'He's down seeing a specialist in the hospital,' she corrected, shooing the children away.

'Hello! I'm Paul from the office . . .'

For a moment she looked as if he'd just announced himself as a child molester.

'Oh, the archeeteck! I've heard him talk about you. I'm Danny's wife. Pleased to meet you.'

They shook hands.

'I was just passing and I thought . . .'

'He'll be sorry he missed you,' she said, moving him purposefully back down the path to the gate.

'Is he keeping all right?'

'Up and down. Y'know.'

Paul felt he was being moved along at an unseemly pace. Bums rush came to mind. When they reached the gate, he paused.

'Beautiful place here.' He looked around.

'Oh, it does.'

He noticed a horsebox at the side of the garage.

'Have you horses?'

She looked uncomfortable. 'Oh, just one or two . . . for the children, like.'

Craning over her shoulder, he glimpsed four of them grazing in the field behind the house.

'Tell him I hope he's better soon!'

'I will.'

As he drove away, he tried to piece it all together: horses, big house, even bigger extension – all on a clerk of works' salary!

Oh, shit, no!

That evening Mary phoned. She was hysterical. She'd just received a letter containing a cat's eyeball and a photo of Sambo as before, but this time with a bandage over one eye. The police had checked with a vet and it definitely was a cat's eye.

'Jim vomited when he saw it,' she wailed.

So Ryan was still sniffing around. At least she'd somebody to turn to. He was glad of that. He was no use to her living a mile away. And as for poor Sambo . . . his blood pressure soared whenever he thought about it.

Brickies. He hated them all.

29

No sooner had Tony stormed out of Steve's room than he regretted it. Useless arsehole as he was, the bastard probably had the power to do him harm. The more he thought about it, the worse he felt. Being sacked would mean disaster. He still had a mortgage, and the three kids to put through third-level education. He had handed himself on a plate to Steve. If the chips were down, even the union couldn't back him over a breach of regulations. He was getting weary of it all. Weary of everyone expecting him to step forward, expecting him to take the flak, while they talked about him behind his back. He could live without that. He could live without work where accountants were dictating the design. He could live without having to clock in like a machine every morning. He could live without all of that. But he couldn't live without the money.

'Steve's written a memo about you,' said Pam.

He had told her his troubles and asked her to poke around, find out what was happening.

'Who to?'

He held his breath.

'Couldn't see the name clear. He tried to hide it. Looked like Johnson, though.'

He was fucked.

*

Danny. Paul couldn't get him out of his mind. He believed the child rather than the mother. Too keen to get rid of him. And then all those trappings of wealth! He was shocked. Danny on the take! He couldn't believe it. Wouldn't believe it. There had to be an explanation.

The men on site weren't unhappy with the clerk of works' absence. Quite the reverse. Less hassle for them. And happiest of all were the plasterers. They enquired after his health.

'That wee hoor dead yet?'

Paul didn't respond.

'No, seriously.' He didn't look serious. 'How is he?'

'OK'

'Tell'm we're prayin for him.'

'Prayin it's nothin trivial,' said another, grinning.

'He'll be touched to know you miss him.' He couldn't resist a smile.

'Miss 'im? Sure, we see as much of him now as then.'

'See more of you,' said yet another, 'an' you're only in and out once a week.'

Paul didn't understand. According to Danny, he was never off their backs.

''Course, when he was on site it was only us he tormented. Them other fellas – ' he nodded towards the brickie squads at the other end of the site – 'get away wi' everything!'

The surprise showed on Paul's face.

'Didn't know that, did yeh?'

This was a different Danny.

'Oh, he never bothered those boys more'n he had to ... except maybe when you came on site.'

The other nodded, 'Couldn't blame him, mind. Considerin.'

'Ay. Play tig wi' hatchets, those boys!'

'And then o'course, like ... they looked after him.'

He didn't want to hear this.

'Oh, ay. Did that, all right. Helped him out, y'know . . . With his own bits and pieces round the house.'

Paul saw again the half-built extension, the same bricks as here. The brick paved drive – same as here. The same PVC windows. The horses. The two-year-old Sirocco.

'Oh, ay, conscientious fella, Danny. Believed in taking his work home with him . . . as much as would fit on his truck.'

They laughed and elbowed each other like schoolboys.

Danny! Hs eyes and ears! He felt suddenly alone.

'A truck?'

'For his business.'

'Business . . . He doesn't need a truck for . . .' He paused. The man read his doubts. 'Now you have it,' he said.

Another winked. 'Oh, our Danny's no dozer, so he's not.'

Paul detached himself and teamed up with the foreman for their walk-about. The thought of Danny niggled away at him and he hardly noticed where he was going. When he did look up, it occurred to him that he was at the house where the cripple had put his X. He remembered it was placed on the floor of the tiny rear porch. Curiosity took him around to it. The foreman followed.

He saw it right away. The hairline cracking that told of a screed not properly bonded to its base was plain to see. Up to their old tricks again. So that was it. The cripple must have known and this was some sort of revenge. He stamped on the floor, then began tapping it with a stick. A hollow sound told the story.

'Something not right there, ay?'

The foreman stamped. 'First I've noticed that.'

'It'll have to come up,' said Paul.

This wasn't good news.

'I could run a skim over it. Be good as new,' the foreman offered hopefully.

Paul's incredulous expression gave him his answer.

'Just a thought,' he conceded.

A labourer began attacking the floor with a pick. A few blows and the pick came bouncing back as it hit something unyielding just below the surface.

Paul saw the glint of metal. 'What's that?'

The foreman shrugged his shoulders. 'No ducts or anythin here!'

The debris was removed and a steel lid was revealed. The lid of what appeared to be a container of some sort.

'What the hell is it?' said Paul.

The foreman looked uneasy.

'I wonder, like . . . should we be touchin it?'

But already the labourer was levering the lid off.

The foreman was first to look in. 'Aw, holy fuck!'

They all stared in.

'Aw, Jesus!' said Paul.

The container was crammed with rifles, their shape just discernible within a thick cocoon of grease and polythene wrapping.

'Aw, Jesus!' he said again.

Runian and Maguire and the foreman and everyone on site denied all knowledge of it. The squad that had worked on that section had quit shortly after. The names and addresses they had given were checked out by the police. False. But still they weren't happy. Wasn't there a full-time clerk of works employed on site, and an architect holding regular inspections?

'You couldn't be up to them fellas,' said the foreman. 'You'd need to be standin beside them every minit o'the day! Clerk of works can't be everwhere.'

If the plasterers were to be believed, Danny certainly wasn't doing that.

★

That night two policemen visited Paul's flat. The same two as before.

'Well, well . . . the catman! So this is where you are!'

They'd never called with him before. He saw their eyes darting round the room behind him, casing the joint. Did they think he had Sambo!

'Any news?'

The policemen looked at each other.

'News?' said the fat one.

'About the cat?'

'What? Oh, the cat, sir!' He looked slyly at his companion. 'Keeping an eye out for it, sir.'

They tittered.

'Sorry, sir. Just my little joke. No, it's not about that. It's the matter of the arms find on your site. Can we come in?'

The way he said 'your', Paul immediately felt under suspicion. He hadn't a clue what for. It was a reaction bred in the genes. His had been a law-abiding family; if policemen called at your house, you must have done it – simple as that.

They shouldered their way past him into the living room and sprawled across his settee.

'There's unhappy people out there,' said the fat one.

'Seriously unhappy,' echoed his pal. 'Unhappy at losing those guns. Know what I mean?'

He thought he did.

'Why tell me?'

'They're lookin for somebody,' said the fat one.

'Who?'

'An informer.'

Paul suddenly felt cold.

'Me?'

'*We* know it's not you, sir,' said the thin one.

Paul noticed he emphasised the 'We'.

'But do they?'

'All we're sayin is . . . be careful, sir.'

'But . . . this is crazy. I mean, what can I do?'

'Just be on your guard, sir.' The way he kept saying 'sir' made Paul even more uneasy.

'But, look . . . I don't know anything about this!'

The policemen looked at each other.

'Nothing?' said the fat one.

'Nothing.'

'Sure?'

'Certain.'

They looked at each other again, as if deciding who should break the bad news.

'We hear different,' said the thin one.

'What?'

'We hear you went straight to the guns.'

'An' what's worse, they've heard it too . . .'

'And they're wonderin. Just like we are.' The fat one grinned at him encouragingly.

Flustered, he looked from one to the other.

'It just . . . just happened!'

'They reckon you were told by somebody,' said the other.

His legs wobbled. He sat down. His heart thumped. His veins flexed themselves for the floodtide.

'Me!' he said.

The cripple. The note. X marks the spot. All flashed before him.

They noted his hesitation.

'Precisely, sir.'

Tony was worried. A week had gone by and no further word from Steve or, more importantly, from Johnson. Every phone call tightened a knot in his stomach. He was jumpy. He wasn't sleeping. His work began to suffer. He began making mistakes.

His wife noticed as well. Eventually he told her what had happened.

'You what?' She stood, open-mouthed.

'"Stick it," I said!' He knew she'd be proud of his manly stance.

She looked at him as if he'd just announced he was a serial killer.

'You eejit!'

'What?'

She shook her head in disbelief, 'Have you no wit? You'll go straight in there tomorrow and make some excuse – any-thing – and apologise!'

'Come off it . . .'

'I mean it!'

'To him?'

'You're always on about how they'd love to get rid of you. You've just obliged!'

'You expect me to crawl to him . . . to Steve?

'Yes.'

'To eat shite?'

'Whatever.'

'Never!' He thumped the table. 'Never!'

'I'm serious, Tony. Y'hear!'

He stood up. Defiant.

She stood up. Equally defiant. 'Fucking serious!'

He sat down. She never swore. He was taken aback.

'Never!' he shouted, not quite as forcefully.

Shite was on the menu first thing next morning when Tony, tail between his legs, entered Steve's office at nine o'clock. He left at nine ten, a much relieved man. Johnson, it seemed, was prepared to overlook his misdemeanour because of his long service, but he would expect him to be much more coopera-tive with management decisions in the future.

Steve had not passed this on, prepared instead to let Tony sweat. He smiled.

'I was getting round to telling you.'

Tony stared across at a face he would never tire of kicking. 'Thanks, Steve.'

He couldn't believe he heard himself say that.

Since the finding of the guns there had been an uneasy feeling about the site. Paul sensed it. Everybody did. The incident was reported in the papers. The police said there might be repercussions and to be on the lookout for anything out of the ordinary. He certainly was. If he hadn't been, he would never have noticed the wellington boots.

Of course he'd been driving past them for months. The two boots sticking out of the mud heap were part of the furniture by now. They had become a feature with Danny's obituary, giving everyone a smile as they passed through the entrance gates. But this morning something was wrong. The label, which had withstood all weathers, now lay a few feet away, and as he slowed the car down he noticed that the boots were on the wrong feet.

Something made him stop. He approached the boots. He lifted one, but instead of finding a brush pole inside he found an upended crutch.

His legs went weak.

For a second he thought of just walking away. But he couldn't. His legs wouldn't move.

He reached out for the other boot.

As he withdrew it from its support, he turned aside and vomited.

A mangled human leg, black and stiff in death, poked skyward from the mud.

'Jinxed, that site!' said Ken. 'You've done your share, Paul.

We'll put somebody else on it. There's lots of rehab work needing done.'

Even Stella showed interest in the news. It wasn't every day you found a dead body on your site. A murdered body. It summed up for her the unfortunate circumstances that architects had to work with. These things happened when you rubbed shoulders with the lower orders.

'I wouldn't stay there another minute, mixing with people like that,' she said.

'Nor I,' said Ken.

'That poor man,' said Val.

'Those who live by the sword die by the sword,' said Stella.

She was starting to bug even Val. 'But you know nothing about him,' Val protested.

'They're all up to something, believe you me.'

Paul was shaken. Somebody on the site, somebody he rubbed shoulders with regularly, must have had a hand in this. He'd told the police all he knew, about the cripple and the brickies, the cat, everything. They said he might be in danger himself, as the ones who'd killed the cripple might think he had talked more than he had. But even with that, Paul wasn't going to give up the site. He wasn't going to go back to the awful rehab work – Mr Brown wafted pungently to mind. And anyway, all this was supposition.

He turned to Tony: Tony would support him. 'What do you think?'

Tony looked at him. 'Me?'

'What would you do?'

Tony dropped his eyes. Anything he said would be sure to find its way back to Johnson, via that arse Ken.

'To be honest, Paul – and I'm not meaning to take away from your stand – I think I'd call it a day. If it was me, like.'

He saw the hurt in Paul's eyes. He knew Paul looked up to

him, knew he expected him to back his stand. But he couldn't; he was on borrowed time with Johnson.

'Let's face it ... it's a madhouse, that site, Paul. Why give yourself all that hassle? How bad has it to get?'

Et tu, Tony? Paul felt as if the rug had been pulled from under him.

'I thought you'd understand,' he said. Then he turned away and headed back to his work station.

The police had given Runian a bad time. They'd turned over his office, gone through his books, checked all the men on the site, but turned up nothing other than a few doing the double. Yes, the dead man had been one of his employees, but he'd been injured in some punishment beating and hadn't come back to the site again. No, he didn't know any-thing about that; he'd just heard it talked about. The guns ... that was anybody's guess. Yes, they could have been hidden by his employees, or they could have been put there by someone coming onto the site when everyone had gone home. Yes, he had site security, but one man couldn't be everywhere at once, and anyway, wasn't the country awash with armed gangs? Everything was covered. But all the time this investigation was going on, his site was stopped and he was losing money.

And the stress of it all was telling on his nerves. He seemed to be thwarted at every turn. He wondered if it was worth carrying on in the building game. He couldn't even choose the men he wanted to work for him. He'd told the council all his problems: how he couldn't get proper tradesmen; how he had to employ only those whom Frank Moriarty supplied, and they were useless. He'd even set up a secret meeting between Moriarty and Johnson, so that Johnson could explain how the lack of proper tradesmen meant work having to be redone, and how those delays were hurting

Moriarty's own community. Moriarty said everything would be fine only for this fussy architect – and anyway, if his men weren't to work on that site, nobody else would work there. End of story. Johnson said it was a tricky business to move an architect without good reason. The union wouldn't wear it. And there the matter had rested.

But now, in the privacy of the builder's hut, Moriarty had a proposal.

'I'll move him for you.'

Runian stared at him. His brother-in-law's cold, matter-of-fact tone made him shiver.

'Now, there'll be none o'that, Frank.'

'He's puttin out your light!'

'Fuckin is too,' said the foreman.

Frank leaned forward. 'And there's another thing. There's politicians really worried about this site. And I mean *really* worried.'

'This site?'

'All of them, but this one most, 'cause it's such a big one.'

'How'd you hear that?'

'Johnson.'

'Gets around, him.'

'Has to if he wants anythin built in this town. He knows nothing happens without the people. His type have to listen. It's people power these days. That's us: the risen people! Power from the streets up.'

Runian snorted. 'What a world, ay!'

Moriarty glared at him. 'What's that mean?'

'Nothin.'

'The council's depending on this site to spend their budget by the end of the financial year. If it doesn't happen, they'll get less money next year. Black mark, see.'

'Be a lot handier if I could just pick my own workforce.'

Moriarty gave him a warning look. 'It's not reality.'

'Reality is I've ten squads of brickies out there who are fuckin useless.'

'I got you those squads!'

'An' aren't I friggin sorry!'

Moriarty glared.

'They're not brickies. Their only qualification is they've all done time – and not at bricklayin!'

Moriarty spread his hands. 'See the big picture, man! Rehabilitation an' all that. Keep people employed. Off the streets. All helps the peace process. These things are important.'

'Not as important as knowin how to lay fuckin bricks!'

'What about social responsibility? What about 'Am I my brother's keeper?'

'I've my own rules.'

'Always took you for a religious man.'

'Desperate times, desperate measures.'

'What's that mean?'

'Means I'm gonna do what I have to do.'

'You're talkin through yer arse!'

'I'm thinkin of a few changes.'

'Like?'

'I need proper tradesmen. Not ex-cons.'

Moriarty drew himself up. 'Ex-political prisoners, y'mean!'

Runian refused to be cowed. He gazed out of the window across the site to where clouds of white dust were gusting out of dark window openings.

'Good workers, the plasterers. Nothin needs redoin when they do it.'

Moriarty followed his gaze. 'You don't need plasterers!'

'Did I say I did! Not talkin about plasterers. A couple of brickie squads – neighbours of theirs – have come home from England.'

Frank sat up. 'Now, Leo!'

'Seems they're lookin for work.'

'I'm tellin yeh, don't do it! There'll be trouble.'

'I'm in trouble already.'

'I'm talkin *trouble*. Y'understand?'

'You tellin me how to run my business?'

'Just explainin the facts of life.'

Runian stared him out. 'Is that a threat?'

Moriarty jabbed his thumb to his breast. 'Me?' He had a look of mock surprise. 'Would I threaten you?'

'Frank?'

'Yeah?'

'Piss off!'

30

A NEW POST HAS BEEN CREATED IN HOUSING MANAGEMENT WHICH WILL ACT AS A LIAISON WITH THE ARCHITECTS' DEPARTMENT. THE PERSON SOUGHT MUST BE A QUALIFIED ARCHITECT, ETC. . . .

Pam landed the flyer on Paul's desk with her accustomed thump.

'No good you boys applying. You have to know what liaison means!'

He was still reading it when the phone rang.

'Seen it?' It was Joan.

'Pardon?'

'The job!'

'Oh, the job? Yes, just reading about it now.'

'Good. Look, the thing is to get your application in right away, in case you forget.'

This concern for his career prospects warmed him. A concern above and beyond the call of duty. Maybe it would attach itself to other areas.

'Joan . . .'

'Look, I'm sending you the form. I know the head of personnel.'

He felt that he was being carried along on her enthusiasm.

'Thanks. But . . .'

'It's no trouble, Paul. Personnel are working closely with us on this appointment.'

'Thanks. It's not about the job . . .'

A silence.

'Oh?'

'No. It's just . . . I was wondering . . .'

This was his big moment.

'Yes, Paul?'

Go for it.

'I was wondering if you've seen that new Mike Leigh film at the MGM?'

It rushed out in a controlled panic. He held his breath. The panic grew. There was a breathing silence at the other end. He fell into it.

'It's just a thought. I mean, y'know, whatever. Doesn't matter if . . .' He trailed off into a jibbering wimper.

'Oh, I'd like to Paul . . .'

His hopes soared.

'. . . but . . .'

Then crashed.

'. . . I've such a heavy schedule this week. I'd need to see my diary. Can I ring you?'

Not an outright dismissal. Hope still lived.

For the first time in ages Steve had left his drawer unlocked. He was usually careful, locking it even if he went out to the toilet. Pam looked around – he was at a meeting somewhere, and she hadn't had a good rummage in ages. She opened the drawer. And there it was, his black book of misdeeds. Time for a bit of updating.

She began to read.

'No way! That's not for an architect . . . a desk job! An

architect wants to be where it counts, on the site. Right, Paul?'

Tony was giving out about the proposed new post.

'Right,' said Paul. But his voice lacked the conviction it once had.

'In the muck and mire of reality, dealing with real problems, real people. Right?'

'Don't know about that,' said Ken. 'Wouldn't cost me a thought, leaving all those whingeing tenants behind.'

'That's your fellow man you're talking about,' said Tony.
'Scumbags!'

'What've you against them?'

'Bad taste for starters. They all wear those stupid baseball caps back to front and have moustaches and tattooed arms. And the men are worse.'

'Gas chambers! That's the answer,' said Paul.

Ken glared at him.

'They're human beings, for Christ's sake!' said Tony.
'Scumbags.'

'Takes one to know one,' said Paul.

They all looked at him.

Later Tony took Paul aside. Told him Ken could write a bad report on him. Could sink him.

Paul shrugged. 'Ken and I've an understanding.'

'He's your team leader. He's got the upper hand.'

'But I've the lower one – and it's round his balls!'

A week had passed and Joan hadn't rung. Paul's spirits drooped. He felt lonely, rejected. He felt old. Everything was against him. Even Tony seemed to have gone soft on him. He had no support from his superiors; it was all getting too much. Did anybody else get this hassle?

Out of interest, he went onto one of Tony's sites. And he was shocked. There was all the slipshod work that he wouldn't allow on his own site! Was he the odd one here? What the hell was he killing himself for? Maybe he should be like all the rest, just turn a blind eye for an easy life. Or leave. But, then, he liked working in the public sector. It felt good doing something worthwhile for your disadvantaged fellow man, provided he kept his distance.

There was the other option, of course: Joan's job. This would keep him in the council, would keep him in touch with housing, but would remove him from the daily stresses of site supervision. The idea began to grow on him.

When the application form arrived, he filled it in right away.

At seven thirty in the morning, the building site was at peace. No cranking machinery, cursing men, hammering, sawing. From the surrounding streets the odd rattle of a milkman on his rounds. Only birdsong and the fluttering of polythene cover sheets. Increasingly Runian had begun to appreciate these moments: peaceful oases in his fraught life. He made a point of always being first on the site and last to leave at night. That way little escaped his notice. Today he was especially early.

A roar of engines announced the arrival of the plasterers and their friends. First the blue van of the plasterers, then another blue van: the new brickies back from a job in England. Even at rest the vans quivered and creaked after the stress of the long country journey. They were doing eighty and ninety miles an hour along narrow country roads until they hit the motorway and then they really opened up. Bits of hedge and gorse were caught under bumpers and wheel trims. The striations of a million smashed insects streaked the bodywork and windows.

The men disgorged themselves, stamping and stretching cramped limbs, groaning and laughing alternately.

'My arse feels like it's somebody else's!'

'One hoor of a journey, that!'

'It'll be shorter on the way back.'

'We'll only owe you half the petrol then.'

'Wouldn't you love to believe it. You're as mean as cat shit, you!'

'Listen to scatter-the-cash there! Saw him in the pub the other night throwin money round like a man with no arms!'

Runian stepped forward.

'Ah ha! And here's the boss himself, boys. Meet Mr Runian!' The foreman plasterer did the introductions.

'Give me a fair day's work for a fair day's pay and we'll get on fine, men,' said Runian.

'Can't ask fairer than that,' said the new foreman brickie.

'Just one thing. You're strangers here. There's things goin on roundabout you don't know about, an' you don't want to know about. Belfast's a strange place, as I'm sure you're aware. Just keep doing your work and don't bother with anybody and you'll be fine.'

'One question, boss?'

Runian could see he was the joker of the party, the way the others tittered and nudged each other in anticipation.

'Right.'

'Do the Belfast women wear bulletproof knickers?'

'You'll find that out for yerselves.'

They liked that.

'And another?'

'A serious one now?'

'About money.'

'OK.'

'If we're blown up, will we be docked the time we're in the air?'

★

Tony had had the frighteners put on him all right. Put on him by Steve – and he hated him for it. And he hated himself even more. But he was over a barrel, so he just kept his head down, steering well away from any union problems which might bring him into confrontation with Johnson.

But he felt a shit. Paul hardly spoke to him now. He knew he felt let down. He wanted to clear the air, to explain himself. Talking to him privately in the office was impossible, so he decided to visit him in his flat that night to sort things out.

His first surprise came when the flat door opened.

'Pam!'

'Tony!'

'God!'

Pam shouted into the flat. 'You'll never guess who's here!'

Paul came into the hall.

'Jesus!'

'No. Just me,' said Tony.

'Come in! Pam, stick the kettle on!'

'If you ask me nicely.'

'Please?'

She moved towards the kitchen.

Paul nodded after her. 'It's not what you think, y'know.'

'Have I said a word?'

'It's not even what you're not thinking.'

Tony was still absorbing this when the phone rang. Pam, passing, went to answer it.

Paul glanced at his watch. 'Leave it!' he shouted.

Pam froze. 'Him?'

It kept ringing.

Paul turned to Tony. 'Will you do something for me Tony? Will you answer that?'

'This a trick?'

'Go on!'

'Not gonna bite me, is it?' He put the phone to his ear.

The voice was indistinct at first but gradually he was able to pick out the words from the background sounds of a noisy bar. He wished he hadn't.

'Listen well, fucker! Remember that cripple fella? Well, that's nothin to what we'll fuckin do to you, you fuckin bastard. We'll cut your balls off with a rusty blade . . .'

He slammed the phone down. He looked at Paul. 'Your mother?'

'That's regular, maybe three times a night.'

'It's still going on?'

'Never stops.'

Now Tony felt more ashamed than ever. 'Paul, I – '

Paul jumped in, as if reading his mind. 'Look, I know all about Steve.'

'Steve?'

'That's why Pam's here. Came to tell me. Safer than the office. I know all about it. You and him.'

Tony, nonchalantly, 'About what?'

'He's got you, hasn't he? Pam's read his wee black book.'

'Oh.'

'You and Stella. He reckons he's got you both in his pocket.'

'No way!'

'Every loving detail,' said Pam. 'He's got it all down. Times, dates – the lot. Absences from workstation without just cause . . . it's all there.'

Tony felt naked.

'He reckons he's neutered you,' said Paul.

'Me? No way!' But he knew he sounded neutered.

'Blackmail, that's what it is,' said Pam.

Tony went quiet.

Then the big surprise. 'And Stella's told all,' said Paul.

'Stella?'

'About our computer fix,' said Pam. 'It was her ladyship.'

'No!'

'Oh, a right wee informer she's turned out to be. Tells him everything.'

'Why?'

'Same as you. Caught her skiving off. Said he would tell on her if she didn't say what she knew about our production figures. She spilled the beans.'

'Has her by the balls,' said Paul.

Tony looked flattened.

Paul had always been a bit in awe of Tony. No longer. He, Paul, now held the moral high ground. It felt right.

Next day he bumped into Mary in the centre of town.

'You a child molester now?' she said.

'What?'

'That young one.'

'What young one?'

'What young one! Back to your old tricks, ay?'

'Don't know what you're talking about!'

'Look, I don't care. Makes no difference to me who you lure up to your flat!'

'Y'mean last night?'

'Needn't deny it. I was going to call and I saw her going in. Didn't want to interrupt your little tête-à-tête.'

'It was Pam out of the office, for God's sake! Credit me with some taste please.'

'Taste? Huh! Remember, I've seen that Claire slut.'

'Mary!'

'As I said, I don't care. I'm happy for you and your harem! Goodbye!'

She turned and strode away.

'Why'd you call?' he shouted after her.

'Oh, nothing worth interrupting your groping for.'

'Mary?'

'Just ... a firm offer's been made on the house. If you're interested.'

He felt sick.

Next day in the office, Paul's mind was occupied with the implications of the impending sale of the house. The final curtain on twenty years of marriage. He'd read somewhere that divorce and moving house were, after bereavement, the two most stressful life events. He was having them both together. His blood pressure must be off the Richter scale by now. He was about to arrange a doctor's appointment when the phone rang. His stomach knotted. Probably more abuse. He could never get used to it. He lifted the receiver.

'Architects' department. Paul speaking.'

Silence. The abusers were never silent.

'Hello?'

Still silence. Could only be one person. Danny was back.

'Danny?'

'Right.'

'Well, how are you?'

'Survivin.'

'I called out to see you but ...'

'I heard.'

'Sorry I missed you.'

'No harm.'

Silence.

'Still there Danny?'

'Doin anythin?'

'Y'mean now, like?'

'Ay.'

'Nothing particular.'

'Need a word.'

'OK.'

'See you in the Dummy Fluter.'

'OK. When?'
'Half an hour.'
'OK.'
Click.

There is always something deliciously guilty about drinking in a pub in the middle of the morning when everyone else is working, particularly when you have a job to go back to. Paul felt it as soon as he stepped over the entrance. He felt his cares and woes slip from him in the magic of low lights, sparkling tiles, burnished brass rails and fittings. But if the tiles sparkled, the customers didn't. Mid-morning drinkers – and they are mostly men – are rarely happy drinkers. They have time on their hands while others are making money; time to worry about their wives, other men's wives, money, drinking, life, the troubles and much else besides.

There weren't many at the bar. He couldn't see Danny at first, then he noticed him beckoning from one of the snugs around the walls. He greeted Paul with a sheepish smile. A glass of orange juice sat on the table in front of him. Even in the gloom of the snug, he looked surprisingly healthy, with the glow of an outdoor existence about him; not at all like a man who had been off on extended sick leave. He had risen from the dead in the pink of condition.

He started up. 'Drink?'

Paul put out a restraining hand. 'Can't go in breathing fumes this hour of the day.'

Danny sat down again. He didn't speak. Nor did it look like he was going to. Whatever was coming obviously needed time to gestate. It seemed that it would be hard going. Paul felt he had to crank-start him.

'Getting about again, then?'

Danny shrugged.

'What is it?'

Danny looked up. 'What?'

'Whatever's wrong with you.'

'Oh, that.'

'Serious, is it?'

'Bangor Reserves.'

'What?'

'Nerves.'

'Oh.'

He knew it. He was right. Danny just hadn't been himself lately.

'Least that's what it says on the certificate.' He gave something close to a sly smile. 'Truth is, needed a break.'

Paul was shocked at the admission.

'You weren't sick?'

'Oh, I was,' said Danny. 'Sick of that place. Sick of that bloody site!'

Passion. This wasn't Danny!

Danny shook his head at the unspoken rebuke. 'I know what you're thinkin. But you're wrong.'

'Danny, I . . .'

Danny leaned across the table at him. He looked around before he spoke.

'Leanin on me.'

Paul dropped his voice.

'Who?'

'The quare fellas.'

'What?'

'Them ones.'

'Who?'

'Y'know.'

His habit of speaking in riddles was driving Paul mad.

'For God's sake, Danny!'

'Frank Moriarty's men.'

'Moriarty? But he . . .'

'Nobody works on that site unless he's come through Moriarty.'

'But what's he to do with you?'

Danny gave him a questioning look. 'You've heard about Moriarty?'

'I've heard about him . . . sort of.'

'Believe me, it's all true. He knows all these boyos . . . these so-called paramilitaries. He's everybody's friend, their agent sort of. He does deals for them . . .' Once again he looked about him. 'He's the reason I'm on the sick.' He leaned even closer. 'Started puttin pressure on me. Heard I was buildin an extension. Next thing Runian's offerin me bricks, cement, timber, PVC windows, doors, a conservatory – the lot . . .'

'A bribe?'

'Sort of. Y'see . . . normally the clerk of works gets offered bits and pieces to keep him sweet – nothin much, a bag of cement maybe or a bit of timber. Harmless stuff. But this was big-time. And the thing is, I didn't need the bloody stuff. See, I do a bit of contractin myself – on the side, like. As you'd a seen, I'm not stuck for a bob or two. And when I started refusin the stuff it just kept turning up at my house anyway. So what do you do? I used it. And then of course, once I'd used it, I was reminded of it every so often. Just so's I'd know what was what.'

'Blackmail. Trying to buy you?'

'I come a lot dearer than that.'

He felt better about Danny already.

'Trouble was, they thought they'd bought me. So when I started doin my job, turning down bad work and stuff, they thought I wasn't playin the game. Their game. Anyway, the upshot was I started gettin hints on site what might happen to me if I didn't do so and so.'

'Threats?'

'Then the phone calls started.'

'Go on.'

'Callin me all sorts. Well, I could handle that. But then my wife would lift it and she'd get it too. That was the worst part. Didn't like that. Not one bit.'

'Scum!'

'So I got offside. Nobody bought me. That's what I want to tell you. No matter what you might hear different.'

'Never doubted that,' he lied.

'Also I'm sorry you were left in the lurch. I wouldn't have done it if I'd known you weren't getting a relief clerk of works.'

Paul shrugged. 'I've managed.'

'Too well, it seems . . .'

Paul looked up.

'You've annoyed a lot of people.'

'Good,' said Paul.

'I've heard things.'

'What?'

'Things.'

'Well?'

'There's a big fallout coming.' Again he leaned forward and looked round. 'Runian's fired the local men, Moriarty's men, and brought more of the countrymen in. Brickies this time. Frank Moriarty's not happy. His men aren't happy. And when they're not happy, you gotta look out.' He sat back. 'That's it. That's all I wanted to say. Just watch out for yerself.' Then he stood up, said, 'Bye!' and was off out through the door before Paul could gather himself.

He sat for a few minutes, wondering where all this was leading. Then, as he went to stand up, his shoulder was gripped from behind, forcing him back down again. Turning, he saw a tattooed arm projecting from an egg-stained T-shirt. Above it was an angry face. A drunk face. It rang a bell. Ding-dung, it said.

'Hey you ... archeeteck ... Phrase fuckin one I was told!'

Return of the shite monster!

He wasn't in the mood for him.

'I've wrote to my MP about yous lot. And my councillor down at the city hall is gonna get on to your boss. And I've wrote to the papers ... An' my fuckin toilet still isn't fixed ... Hey! Hey, where you goin?'

Paul stood up. He checked the dog wasn't about.

The man swayed, acting the big fella in front of his mates. 'Yous are public servants. I want some fuckin service. Y'hear? Ay?'

The whole bar was looking. How to retreat with dignity?

He turned and faced the enemy. 'Oh dear! Off your medication again?'

'Wha ...'

'Stay right there! I'll just get the nurse and she'll take you back home.'

He walked calmly to the door. Then ran.

Runian and Maguire relaxed. Since the new country brickie squads had started, production had at least doubled. Money was coming in again. It meant the programme being caught up. It meant pressure being eased. By happy chance, most of the squads they'd fired had got other work right away, so there was no trouble from Frank Moriarty. Runian's gamble in a fit of pique had paid off. Took people to stand up to these boyos from time to time. Thought they ran the friggin world. Everything was falling into place. So it came as a surprise when two policemen came into the hut.

'Good day, sir!'

Runian started. The sight of the tall black uniforms, the shiny peaked caps, the gleaming, creaking black leather belts and gun holsters always sent a chill through him. Black enamelled bastards, that was what his old fella called them every time they carted him off to jail for the duration of a royal visit. He raced over the litany of his own more constitutional misdemeanours that lurked at the back of his brain.

The policeman seemed to read his mind. 'Nothing to worry about, sir. Hopefully.'

That mock formal address always unnerved him.

'Look, those guns and the murder, all that stuff – we've been through it all.'

'Not that, sir.'

His confidence started to return. 'So what's your problem, then?'

'Oh, not my problem, sir.'

'What, then?'

'Your problem.'

'What?'

'Just a word of warning, sir.'

'Warning?'

'There's been a car with four men aboard hanging around your site these last few days.'

'Oh?'

'Name of McCann mean anything? Known to his mother and others as Genghis?'

'Can't say it does.'

'Bad boys, these. Had any problems lately?'

Runian and Maguire looked at each other. Runian shrugged. 'Well, we fired a lot of men a while back. But there's been no aggro. Nothing.'

'No. Not those. We know about them. These are different.'

'How different?'

'Let's say ... a rival faction. Seem to be paying a lot of attention to your site.'

The policemen turned and stooped to leave the hut.

'Just keep an eye out, sir. That's all.'

31

Stella wasn't happy with her role. Informer. She didn't shy away from the word; that, after all, was what she was. And if it took that to keep her job, so be it. Anyway, she'd never felt any great bond with the others; they weren't really her type. Steve was blackmailing her, it was as simple as that. He'd ring down and ask to be updated with what was going on in the architects' office. Lately, though, she hadn't much to tell him. Even Tony wasn't his usual bolshie self. The upshot was she hardly ever had any contact with her tormentor other than passing on the stairs or in the corridors. And that suited her fine.

So it came as a shock when she opened the door into the print room – and there he was. Alone. She was about to back out, but he turned and saw her.

'Only be a tick. Come on!'

'Look ... I'll come back later. Other things ...' she flustered.

He whipped up a sheet from the machine. 'Finished!' He beckoned her forward.

She came reluctantly.

'Pam's out today, so I've to do my own bloody photocopying.' He stepped aside to let her at the machine. He made no moves to leave the room.

'Very hot in here, isn't it?' he said. 'Why don't you take your jacket off?'

As she tried to order her sheets, she fumbled. His presence made her clumsy. She dropped some papers. Immediately he stooped down and retrieved them for her.

He grinned. 'Dear me, is that the effect I have on you!'

She smiled an inane smile.

He moved closer. She could smell him now, his BO fighting a losing battle with his halitosis.

'I'm glad our little arrangement works so well. Everything works so much more smoothly, thanks to you.'

She shifted away. He followed. The smell of his aftershave was now adding to the fug. It was overpowering, subduing all other odours. She thought she might throw up.

'I was wondering, Stella, maybe sometime we could go for a drink. Just a quiet drink. Have a talk.'

Oh, God, no! She'd stop this here and now.

'Steve, to be perfectly honest . . .'

Then he pounced. He was all over her. Hands groping. His mouth clamped on hers. His body grinding into her, flattening her against the photocopier. She was in shock. She couldn't move. She was rigid. She couldn't shout.

'Really want this, don't you. Ay? Course y'do. I know you do.'

Then the fight came into her. And she exploded in a screaming, punching, kicking, biting frenzy. Her teeth caught his lower lip and ripped it. He sprang back, eyes wide in pain, his hand to his mouth.

'You bitch . . . you fuckin bitch!' His voice growing in outrage each time he brought a bloody hand away from his mouth. 'Look what you've fuckin done to me . . . you . . . you . . . !'

He stopped.

In the doorway, watching, stood Paul.

★

The table in the site hut was covered with drawings, progress charts, bills of quantities, order dockets, receipts. Hunched around these were Runian, Maguire and the foreman. Maguire dabbed away at his calculator. Runian watched him.

'Excellent!' He showed the final figure to his boss. 'We're breaking even. Well, well!'

Runian smiled. 'Who'd a believed it, ay!'

'Fierce workers, those country boys. I'll say that for them. Fierce altogether,' said Maguire.

'Shoulda had them all along,' said the foreman.

'Done as much in a week as those other wankers did since the start,' Runian agreed.

'Frank Moriarty wasn't doing you any favours there,' said Maguire.

'Useful as a man short, him.'

There was a knock at the door. A polite knock. They looked at each other. Nobody on the site knocked politely. Runian nodded to the foreman, and he and Maguire addressed themselves to their paperwork again.

The foreman ambled over and he had just reached the door when it and he were slammed back against the wall of the hut.

Two large men filled the doorway.

'Bit stiff,' said the larger of the two, nodding at the door. 'Could do wi' a bit of oil.'

The other lifted his boot and smashed it through one of the panels. 'Know a good builder could fix that?'

Runian started up. 'What's goin on here . . .'

He got no further. The smaller of the two men produced a gun from inside his jacket and put two fingers across his lips.

'We'll do the talkin.'

He placed the gun on the table. Runian, Maguire and the

foreman stared at it. The man then went and stood with his back to the door, blocking all escape.

The tall one came over to where all the carefully laid-out papers and documents were displayed. The three backed away. With one motion of his arm, he swept everything onto the floor. He then hopped up and settled himself in the cleared space, rocking his legs to and fro, hands firmly grasping the edge.

'Right,' he said, surveying the three men. 'We've got some brickie squads needin work.'

'Look, I told Frank Moriarty – '

'Fuck Frank Moriarty!'

'But Frank . . .'

'Fuck 'im, I said! You're dealin wi' me now.'

'And who are you?' ventured Maguire.

The man at the door placed his hand on his companion's shoulder with an air of reverence. 'Show respect, you! You're talkin to the president of our party. That's who you're dealin with now.'

The president smiled and wiped his nose on his sleeve. He looked around the hut. Then suddenly stopped smiling. Something on the far wall had caught his attention. He stared fixedly at it. All eyes followed his gaze. The object of his interest was a calendar advertising concrete pipes, at the top corner of which was a tiny Union Jack signifying the product's country of origin. His eyes narrowed. From somewhere deep within his diaphragm a whirring noise started to build. It rose in volume and intensity, travelling up his body until it reached his neck, when, throwing his head back, he hawked a great mucous globule of phlegm across the room. A direct hit. The globule struck and quivered on top of the flag, obscuring it. He smiled again. The president now turned to the business in hand.

'The name's McCann. But it's enough for you to know

I'm not Frank Moriarty, big mouth. All right?'

Maguire retreated into a submissive silence.

'What y'want?' said Runian.

'I heard you're lookin squads of brickies.'

'I've got all I need.'

'Aren't you listenin? I *heard* you're lookin brickies.' He pushed his face forward into Runian's.

'I told you, I've . . .'

The man punched Runian in the face. He fell back into Maguire's arms. Maguire went white.

'Look, gentlemen,' said Maguire, disentangling himself from Runian's limp form, 'I don't think you need me . . .'

'Shut the fuck up, you!'

He turned back to Runian. 'You listening? There'll be six new brickie squads starting Monday morning! You got that?'

Runian wiped the blood from his mouth. 'What am I supposed to do with the country boys?'

'Whatever the fuck y'like.'

Paul hadn't told Pam about the job application. Why should he? Still, he did feel a twinge of guilt. She knew how he felt about Joan. Bound to be tough on her. But she just wasn't in the same class. Anyway, it was only an application. He mightn't get the job. And he wasn't even sure if he wanted it.

Life in the office had become more bearable. Steve was now a spent force. Still obnoxious, but the important thing was he was without power. If there was one thing the union was down on, it was sexual harassment. It was looking for a good solid case to make an example of, and Steve knew this. He knew it because Paul had made a point of telling him. And he told him again and again. He was caught in the act and Paul was the witness. It was only a matter of Stella making a formal complaint for the wheels to be set in motion – then goodbye, Steve.

From now on Steve survived on their sufferance.

Danny was back. He felt bad about leaving Paul in the lurch again. So he came out with his hands up. A surprise awaited him. Good brickwork! The countrymen were a tonic. Like all good workmen, they only did a job once. The site was tidy, with the men having the pallets of bricks neatly stacked and conveniently situated for working; tools and equipment handily arranged, not thrown at their arses. He liked an efficient site. An efficient site was a happy site, he always said. There was no pressure any more, no nasty threats, no midnight phone calls to his home. It was a new era. And it lasted all of a week.

The first Paul knew of the change was Danny's phone call from the site.

'They're back.'

'Who?'

'The quare fellas.'

'Who?'

'Y'know!'

'Danny, I . . .'

'Same as was here before.'

'Frank Moriarty's brickies? Aw, God!' Paul's heart sank.

'No . . .'

It rose again.

'Not exactly.'

Sank again.

'What's that mean?'

'They're not Moriarty's people – but outta the same stable, maybe worse. That's all I know. Hard cases you wouldn't want to fall out with.'

'But what about the countrymen?'

'Gone.'

'What!'

'Sacked. These ones have their jobs.'

'And they just left?'

'You would too. The look o' this lot.'

'What about Runian?'

'No say in the matter.'

'Shit!'

'Back to square one, ay!' Danny's voice was low and despairing.

Paul decided to buck him up. 'Listen, I'm gonna take no more of this nonsense.'

'No choice.'

'But I have. I could take this to the top. I could have the whole bloody site shut down.'

'Serious?'

'Bloody sure I could!'

'Think the big boys'll heed you?'

Paul was working himself up into a lather of righteous indignation. 'Oh, they'll heed me. If I have to go to the top, to the papers, to councillors, to MPs, to whoever.' He stopped. He suddenly realised he was sounding like the shite monster.

'They'll get rid of you.'

'So? There's other jobs.'

There was a silence for a bit before Danny spoke.

'For you maybe.'

'What? Look . . . I'm not involving you in this, Danny.'

'Have to.'

'Why?'

'Need me to back up what goes on on site.'

Paul hadn't thought of this. Of course he was right. His word alone was no good.

'And would you?'

Silence.

'Hello?'

'Have to think about that,' said Danny.

'Danny, I . . .'

Click.

A few days later, when they met on site, Danny was still undecided. He shook his head and scuffed the ground with his toe. 'I wouldn't go outta my way to annoy those boys and that's the truth now.'

He was scared. They stood wordless for a moment.

One of the plasterers emerged from the dusty darkness of the house for a breather. He blinked in the sunlight. Then he looked over to where Danny and Paul stood. A labourer passed by, performing his usual feat of carrying a bag of cement under each arm across the site. As he passed, the plasterer nodded in the man's direction and shouted across at Danny.

'Used to be a brain surgeon,' he said. Then, seeing he'd caught their interest, he jiggled his hand to his mouth. 'The curse of Ireland!' he said, wagging his head.

Paul looked after the labourer, imagining the man's previous existence and his now simple, uncomplicated life. No worries. No responsibilities. No threatening phone calls. Just doing what he was told and asking no questions. Getting his achievement through carrying bags of cement for other men's appreciation. He envied him.

The plasterer noted his interest. 'A great hoor of a man, ay? Brains and brawn – that's how we grows 'em in the country.'

He turned and went back into the house. A great laugh erupted from the darkness.

Danny looked at Paul's wondering face.

'Spoofers!'

Paul laughed an embarrassed laugh. He wanted to believe it.

'Tell you anythin, those boys!' said Danny. Then he
looked down to where the new brickies rose and dipped
behind the rising walls. 'But at least you'd get decent work
outta them. Not like that crowd.'

These new brickies were the same as the old: up to all the
tricks, and short cuts, and whatever they thought they might
get away with. But Paul and Danny were on to them. So
much so that yet again the site was almost at a standstill. That
morning Danny had probed an unusually wide horizontal
bed joint to find that it contained a folded newspaper mortared over in a careless moment. He ordered that that section
of wall – a whole morning's work – be taken down and
rebuilt. As usual, they had plenty to complain about. But it
wasn't that that had brought them to the site that day.

Runian had called a meeting. There was a note of exasp-
eration in his voice on the phone. And when Paul noticed his
black eye and puffed face, he knew something wasn't right.
Nor did the builder seem his usual aggressive self. Maguire,
looking uneasy, sat beside him. To open proceedings,
Runian held up his hands in mock surrender.

'Cards on the table, boys. Right?'

Paul shrugged his shoulders. Danny just stared, unblink-
ing, at Runian.

'You're crucifyin me, boys, I'm tellin you straight!'

He looked from Danny to Paul for a reaction. There was
none.

'Crucifying. It's the right word for it,' seconded Maguire.

'Us?' said Paul.

'Who else?'

'Your brickies for starters! Who wants a house built on a
newspaper – and the *Sun* at that!'

'Right. I know we've problems there. But . . .'

Paul wasn't going to have any more messing about.

'Face it, your workmanship's crap. End of story.'

'Look – ' Runian leaned forward – 'you know my problems here. Right?' He nodded his head inviting their complicity. 'I don't choose the people who work on this site. You live in this town. You know the score. You know that, don't you?' Again the suppliant nodding. 'In normal circumstances, I wouldn't have these people anywhere about me.'

'And you'd be right,' said Danny.

'But what the hell can I do?'

'Simple,' said Paul. 'Just get the countrymen back, or anybody who can lay bricks properly, and your problems'll be over.'

'Think I don't want to?'

'His hands are tied,' said Maguire. 'It's a matter of taking what you can get.'

Paul looked at him. 'Wrong. It's a matter of getting it right! That's all that concerns us.'

Runian leaned forward again. 'Look . . . we're on a knife edge here. Y'understand me?'

Maguire nodded agreement.

'What's that mean?' said Paul.

'What it says.'

'I'm no wiser.'

Runian twisted in his seat. 'I'll be straight. We're havin troubles . . .'

'Fuckin troubles . . .' the foreman added.

'See, these new brickies aren't my choice . . .'

'You understand how things are, old son?' said Maguire.

'Now, to cap it all, I hear Moriarty's men are wantin back again. I've to deal with all that. And then you boys go settin the site two steps back for every one it goes forward!' He looked around, appealing for understanding. 'Gimme a break, will you? It's getting impossible.'

'Fuckin impossible, old son!' concurred Maguire.

It was the first time Paul had heard him curse. He was impressed.

Runian sat back in his chair, both arms stretched out straight in front of him on the table, in a pose of someone about to make a great announcement.

'To tell the truth, I'm thinkin of pullin out of the bloody contract.'

He drew back to see the effect.

Paul didn't flinch. 'It'll cost you,' he said.

Danny allowed himself a slight sneer.

Runian saw. 'Think I bloody wouldn't? I'm tellin you, I don't give a damn. I'll friggin . . . I'll friggin . . .'

'You'll be done for breach of contract.'

Paul's sobering words brought a halt to his gallop. Runian looked at Maguire.

'He's right,' said Maguire.

Runian subsided like a collapsing balloon. 'What can I do?' A humble tone now.

'Your problem,' said Danny.

Paul didn't like kicking a man when he was down. He sensed the builder's genuine depression. He softened his tone. 'See, you're asking us to lower our standards.'

'Look, I'm only – '

'Can't be done. I've a duty to the public.'

Suddenly Runian's mood changed. 'There's a lot people can do when they have to.'

'Sorry?' said Paul.

Runian leaned forward. 'Y'know, there's more than us interested in this site bein complete in time. Big people. Important people.'

'Yes, more than us,' agreed Maguire.

He said it in a tone that hinted that any further enquiry would be useless. Paul sensed a threat.

'What does that mean?'

Runian shrugged his shoulders. 'I'm just sayin.'

'Who, for instance?' insisted Paul.

'You'll see,' said Runian.

'Yes, you'll see, old son,' said Maguire. 'You'll see.'

A week later there was yet another change on site. From his hut window Danny saw five cars screech in. Each car disgorged a number of men. From the first, five carrying guns emerged. They went up to the places where the brickies were working and spoke to each squad in turn. And in turn each squad packed up their tools, got into their cars and left the site. The new men immediately took up the work from where the others had left it and carried on as if nothing had happened.

Moriarty's men were back.

From their dark openings the countrymen peered out at the scene. They talked quietly among themselves, then resumed their work. The ways of Belfast people were beyond them.

The following day Danny sent in a sick line. Nervous-breakdown time.

'Again?' Ken had just heard. 'How long's it for this time?'

'Three weeks,' said Paul.

'Christ's sake!'

'Will I get a temporary clerk of works?'

Ken reached for his biro. 'I'll do a memo right away.'

'I've plenty of those.'

Ken looked up. 'What?'

Paul had had enough of pussyfooting about.

'It's a clerk of works I want, not a friggin memo.'

Ken glared at him. 'You need something,' he said. 'Here, seen this?' It was the latest site progress report. He dropped it on Paul's desk. 'Your site is due to complete in six months' time. It's three months behind!'

Paul's stomach muscles tightened. He always took this as a personal rebuke.

'And you know the reasons,' he retorted.

'Oh, we all know the reasons. But upstairs they don't care about reasons. They just want things done when they're programmed to be done.'

'Not living in the real world, then, are they!'

Paul could see that his refusal to be panicked irked Ken. But why should he feel guilty about matters which were plainly beyond his control?

'Johnson's going mad.'

'Oh dear. Pity.'

'Livid.'

'Let him blame the council, then.'

'The council?'

'Who picks these builders? You pay peanuts you get monkeys!'

He was really getting under Ken's skin now. And he was loving it.

'Would you like to tell him that?' There was a challenging note in Ken's voice.

'I'm happy to say that's your job, Ken.'

Their eyes locked.

'You do know what's at stake here, don't you?' Ken spoke very deliberately.

Paul shrugged his shoulders.

'I see you don't.'

'So what's the mystery?'

'Very important, your site. All the money budgeted for it has to be spent in this financial year. If it isn't, it weakens the council's case for getting more money next year for a huge housing boost to the city. Big politics behind that. More houses mean more jobs, mean more money, mean fewer unemployed young men as fodder for these paramilitary gangs. And if Johnson can – '

'Johnson?'

'Oh, yes, Johnson is Mr Big in all this. See, if he swings it, the powers that be will think the sun shines out of his arse – and he's on his way maybe to a directorship.'

Ken drew back, looking for the effect.

'Well, bully for him!' said Paul.

Ken smiled weakly.

'Pity he didn't get proper builders to spend the money for him!' said Paul.

Ken stopped smiling. He dropped his head. Then he began shuffling his feet.

'I was meaning to talk to you about that . . .'

Paul sensed something was coming.

'Look, an architect has every right to expect the best, but sometimes, just sometimes, it's a matter of having to take what you're given . . . considering the circumstances, like.'

Paul said nothing. Now where had he heard that before?

'This isn't a normal place . . .'

'I'd never have guessed.'

'Well, all I'm saying is . . . can't you . . . sort of . . . ease up? Just a bit?'

Paul stared at him.

'Runian has his problems too, y'know.'

Paul kept staring.

'For the greater good, of course!' added Ken hurriedly.

32

Runian was engrossed in his accounts when the morning mail was dumped on his desk. To his horror, he had discovered he was now paying out more than he was getting in. If he could have got out of this contract he would, but he couldn't. He was trapped. He resigned himself to ploughing on and getting the bloody thing finished as quickly as possible. But with that damned architect on board, it might never happen.

A package poked invitingly from the pile. He pulled it out. All he got these days were bills. Never packages. He lifted it, weighed it in his hands, looked at the postmark: Belfast. He had never got over the childhood excitement of opening parcels. He loved the ritual: the undoing of the sticky tape, the stripping back of the paper, the prising back of the cardboard flaps, the peering in to see what –

That night Runian sat at home watching the news. It was a strange sensation seeing his own office building taped off, like so many other scenes of crime he'd viewed in the past. Policemen and soldiers moved at will through his premises. He had evacuated the place as soon as he noticed the wires and batteries inside the package. A hoax, the TV presenter said. But it was no hoax. The police told him it was a fully made-up bomb with a half-pound of explosives – enough to reduce his building, and him, to rubble. It was complete, except for one vital wire left conspicuously disconnected. A message, the policeman said. But from whom?

Next morning in the post came a hint. A note made up of letters cut out of a newspaper: GET MORIARTY'S BASTARDS OFF THE SITE OR NEXT TIME IT WILL BE FOR REAL.

The president was back in town.

He was surprised at his own calmness. Amazed really. He felt totally in control as he speculated about the whys and wherefores of all this. The president was obviously disgruntled at having his men booted off the site, but that had nothing to do with him. And anyway ... why this? What was wrong with a letter or a phone call? Or even − no matter how unwelcome − a personal visit? But for Christ's sake, a bomb?

Then his hand started to shake. He looked down and realised his calmness wasn't a good sign.

Time he was out of the building game.

The pub was raucus with early-evening drinkers. Those who had come in straight from work and had stayed on were noisy in their leave-taking. The serious drinkers were loud and confident with the comforting thought of a night's imbibing ahead of them. At the back of the pub a bunch of musicians were tuning up, inclining their ears to each other's instruments. It was a place to take you out of yourself, a place where you could relax and forget your troubles.

Paul was sick of work. He'd got another memo from Ken relaying once again Johnson's concerns at the lack of progress on his site. Everybody knew the reasons, but it was easy to shovel the blame down the line. Yes, he was sick of it. For this one night he would leave all thought of work alone.

But it wouldn't leave him alone. As he bit into his first pint of the evening, a face glimpsed out of the corner of his eye stopped him in mid-swallow. A familar face, but one he couldn't put a name to at first. Then it came to him. He recognised him from the television: Frank Moriarty.

He watched him slip into a corner snug. Through the frosted glass, Paul could see that there was someone else already in there. Then a tough-looking character, who walked with a presidential air, detached himself from further along the bar and joined the other two in the snug.

Paul was curious. He slid along the bar to get nearer. He was about to move to another seat, but sat down quickly and turned his back to the room.

Runian had just come in.

The builder stopped in the entrance, scanning the bar. Moriarty's head emerged from the snug. He beckoned. Runian joined the group.

What was going on? First Pam's sighting of Moriarty and Johnson together. Now this. A thought struck him: who was the fourth man in the snug? Could it be Johnson? He slid further along the bar to see as much as he could. As he peered at the smudges behind the frosted glass, he became aware that he had caught the eye of a tattooed skinhead who happened to be in his line of vision.

'Who y'luckin at?'

The neanderthal fixed him with a dangerous glare.

'Nobody.'

The man slowly pulled himself up straight.

'Am I fuckin nobody, then?' The eyes were full of the unappeasable rage of the slighted drunk.

'Sorry! I didn't mean . . .'

The skinhead lurched over, proffering his glass.

'Want this rammed up yer hole?'

Paul declined the invitation and left.

Life was getting really boring for Pam. There was no fun in annoying Steve any more. He was a broken reed, afraid to look a woman in the eye in case the whole house fell in on top of him. These thoughts went through her head as she mixed herself a vodka and orange in the boardroom. Vodka was getting low; about time somebody noticed. Christmas coming up too. Would it be too cheeky to leave a note to that effect, she wondered? Increasingly she had been using her retreat as the boredom level rose. She leaned back in the director's padded leather chair, put her Doc Marten's up on the polished rosewood table and raised the glass to her lips.

A noise.

She swung her legs off the table and listened. The door to the boardroom creaked as it began to open. She shot into the kitchen area. Her heart pounding, she slid down behind the side of the fridge. She had checked the diary. There was nothing scheduled for this time. She listened.

Two voices, a man and a woman. Whispering.

She peeped out.

Holy shit!

At the door Johnson was snibbing the lock. It wasn't easy to do with Joan biting his neck and his free arm massaging her backside. Job done, he turned all his attention to the writhing body twining itself around him. They stood devouring each other with great gasps and sobs, moving all the time in a slow shuffle towards the kitchen alcove.

Pam squeezed herself into a ball as the gasping, snorting, two-headed beast trundled blindly towards her. She braced herself. They were close now. Closer. Now almost beside her. The gasping breaths just above. She closed her eyes. They passed. She opened her eyes. The two engrossed lovers shuffled by, oblivious of their surroundings and leaving a trail of discarded clothes in their wake. They turned into the shower room. By this stage Joan was down to her skirt and bra, and he had his shirt half off. The rest of their clothes soon fluttered to earth. They disappeared into the shower. She heard the cubicle door swing open. Then the rush of the water, then shrieks and laughs.

Now was her chance. She crept forward and risked a look. Two undulating forms were plainly visible through the fast-steaming-up glass. On all fours, she scampered across the room, keeping out of sight. She reached the door, unsnibbed the lock and let herself out. She closed the door quietly behind her.

Danny rang. He was back. All business.

'All fine now.'

'You, y'mean?'

'What?'

'You?'

'Me?'

'Yes. Your health. You better?'

'Me? Oh, I'm OK.' Pause. 'It's about the other.'

'The other?'

'Y'know . . .'

Paul sighed. He had to fill in the bits himself. 'The site?'

'Sort of . . .'

'So what's happened?'

'Big meetin, so I heard.'

'Well?'

'All sorted.'

He sighed again. 'What's sorted, Danny?'

'All that business . . .' A note of irritability was creeping into his voice at Paul's slow uptake. 'Anyway, the meetin's done the trick. Moriarty called it. All the heavy boys. Know who I mean?'

'Where was this?'

'Some pub . . .'

He saw the shapes behind the frosted glass of the snug.

'They said none of them was gettin anywhere with work on the site stopped.'

'Any eejit could see that.'

There was a pause. Then, conspiratorially, 'Heard your man was there too.'

'Who?'

'Your man.'

He almost shouted. 'Who?'

'What's-'is-name. Y'know ... *Your* man.'

Paul was uneasy offering the name over the phone, but Danny's pump needed primed. 'Johnson?' he whispered.

'Spot on!'

So it was him in the snug!

'All smoothed over, they say.'

'Seriously?'

'So I hear.'

'Let's hope.'

'They've agreed a fifty-fifty jobs split. Just want to get the work goin again.'

Paul was on the point of thinking this was good news when he came back to reality.

'Still be the same useless brickies, though, won't there? Same rubbish workmanship, same problems.'

'That's the strange bit.'

'What?'

'Nobody's worried about that.'

'What do y'mean?'

Danny shrugged. 'Just not mentioned.'

'The work'll still have to get my approval. It'll still have to be redone if it's not right.'

'But that's the thing. Seem to think you'll not be here ...'

He stiffened. 'Me? Not here!'

'Talk of a promotion or somethin.'

'What?

'So they say.'

Paul felt a shadow had passed over him.

'Me? A promotion!'

'Sure, isn't it better than a poke in the eye with a pointy stick!'

Paul imagined a sly smile twisting Danny's lips.

The news that yet another admin post was to be created in the computer section annoyed the architects. The most alarming aspect was that it was to be located on their floor.

'Another chief!' said Ken.

'Absolutely ridiculous!' said Stella.

'And one less Indian down here!' said Tony.

They looked at him.

'How come?' said Stella.

'Stands to sense. They're chock-a-block up there. No space. Means there'll have to be room made on this floor. And that means one of us'll have to go. Let's face it, we're of secondary importance.'

They looked around at their crowded condition. There certainly wasn't room for anybody else.

'Go where?' said Stella.

Tony shrugged his shoulders.

Pam had brought the news. She had eyeballed the memo as it was en route between departments. There was even a definite date for the move: one month's time. Seems the wheels were already in motion.

'Means they must have somebody down here in mind already for a move,' said Tony.

'Must have somebody actually signed up,' said Stella.

'Who?' said Ken. 'I'm certainly not going.' He looked about. 'Anyone else got something they wish to share with us?'

'Certainly not me,' said Tony.

'Nor me,' said Stella.

He turned to Paul. 'Paul?'

Paul went red. He'd told nobody he'd even applied for that job. Anyway, that's all it was – just an application.

'He's got a reddner!' said Ken, pointing.

'No . . .'

'Come on!' Ken was delighted at Paul's obvious discomfort.

'Well, it's nothing really.'

'Ah ha! What's that mean?'

'Just – ' he knew it had to come out some time – 'that new post in management . . . I've applied.'

They all looked at him.

'You serious?' said Tony.

'I've only applied, frig's sake.'

Tony looked shocked. 'Management? You!'

'It's more money,' said Stella.

'Don't even know if I'd take it if I got it,' said Paul dismissively. And he meant it.

'A bloody management wanker, Paul! That's not you,' protested Tony.

'Thought I'd just look around . . . y'know. Too much hassle on site lately. It's getting me down.'

'An architect has to suffer for his integrity,' said Tony.

Paul cast his eyes down, humbled by the fine sentiment. Then he thought: what a load of crap! He remembered what he'd seen on Tony's own site. He said nothing.

'Anyway,' said Ken, getting back to the point, 'seems there's nobody here leaving within the next month and yet somebody must be. The plot thickens.'

'Probably just a management cock-up,' said Stella.

'Wouldn't be the first,' said Ken.

They laughed and agreed that that seemed the most

reasonable explanation, and went back to work. All except Pam who had listened and said nothing. Now she came over to Paul's work station and perched herself on the edge of his desk.

'Kept quiet about that job, didn't you?'

He looked up. 'Huh?'

'Never mentioned a thing.'

She looked down at him with a serious face.

'Should I have?' He laughed.

She didn't.

He felt himself going red again. 'I probably won't get it. Anyway, don't know if I even want it.'

'You'd be working with her, wouldn't you?'

'Who?'

'Your girlfriend.'

'Joan?'

'Who else?'

'She's not my girlfriend.'

'Pull the other one! Of course you'd be working with her.'

'Same department, that's all. It was she told me it was coming up. Nice of her, I thought.'

Pam cocked her head and leaned forward. 'Oh ... and when was this?'

'Few weeks ago. Why?'

'Before the official circulation?'

'Ah ... yeah. Suppose so.'

She leaned back. 'Sounds like insider trading.'

'What?'

'Keen for you to get it, isn't she?'

'I wouldn't say that.'

'Oh, I would.' She looked at him. 'I wonder why.'

He blushed more under her stare. 'What are you on about, Pam?'

She suddenly swung her legs off the desk. 'I'm happy for you both.'

She strode off.

All this talk about Joan being his girlfriend! Hadn't even heard from her for a week. Next day he summoned up the courage to invite her out for lunch.

'... if you're not doing anything ...'

He heard her draw in her breath. He had caught her by surprise.

'Well ...'

Her hesitation unnerved him. He fell into the silence.

'Look, it doesn't matter. Maybe you've something on ...'

Another silence. Then.

'Lunch?'

She made it sound like an invite to a ritual disembowelling. He felt like a piece of shit. Why didn't he face it? She just didn't fancy him. Why didn't he let go, give up, admit defeat, look for somebody else? He knew now he really needed somebody. He needed companionship, love, sex – and in that order. He needed someone to share his bed, his meals, his conversation. He hadn't the makings of a born bachelor. He needed somebody and he wasn't afraid to admit it. Since he'd left Mary, there had been a great hollowness to his life. It needed filling.

But he wouldn't beg. Well, maybe just a little.

'Just a quick lunch?'

A pause. Then:

'OK. But it'll have to be a very quick one.' She sounded like a reluctant bone-marrow transplant donor. 'A very quick one, mind.'

And it was. Within twenty minutes they had met, talked – mostly about her and her very important work – eaten, paid and were out on the street again. She apologised but said she had meetings to attend. It was only after she left that he realised she'd headed off every attempt by him to get close. And the only reference to his job application was when she mentioned that he would have a lovely desk by the window – as if he'd already got the job!

Things got stranger a few days later when Pam flounced up to his desk and slapped a memo down.

'Well, you're certainly well in!' She pushed the piece of paper under his nose.

He started to read. 'What . . .'

The memo was from Johnson to Ken. It stated baldly that the new admin monitoring recruit could be located in the space shortly to be vacated by Paul, who would be joining the housing management department in his new role as architectural liaison officer.

He stared at the memo. 'What. . .!'

'You shit!' She spat the words.

He looked up.

'You friggin shit! You've got that job and you never said a word.'

He shook his head. 'It's a mistake! Must be.'

'So you're a liar too.'

He waved his arms about in helpless protest. 'It's mad! It's a mistake. It's rubbish!'

'Mistake,' she sneered.

Her venom amazed him. A woman scorned. But now he started to get angry.

'Why are you so annoyed anyway?'

'Y'know I can't stand liars.'

'Look . . . I know nothing about this.'

'How can Johnson say – '

'How do I know! I haven't even had an interview or any-thing. How can I have got the friggin job!'

She stopped in her tracks. 'No interview?'

'See! It's stupid.'

She thought about it. 'Honest?'

He turned the memo in his hand. 'It's mad.'

'Obviously Johnson doesn't think so,' she said, but there was no venom any more.

'Pam, I'm telling you, I know nothing about it.' He saw her considering this. Why the hell should he care what she thought? But he wouldn't want her to think him a liar. 'As true as God! Scouts' honour! Whatever! I haven't a clue.'

She took back the memo. Calm now.

'Maybe I've a clue,' she said.

'What?'

She stood up. 'That's for you to find out. Ask your girl-friend.'

She flung the words over her shoulder as she walked away.

Jealous as hell!

He smiled. Yes, he still had what it takes. Pity it was wasted on Pam, though.

'Of course you've got the job, Paul.' Joan seemed surprised at the question.

'What?'

'Of course you have.'

He imagined her smiling at the other end of the phone.

'But the interviews . . .'

'Oh, there'll be interviews, all right, but Brian – Mr Johnson – says it'll just be a matter of form. You stand head and shoulders above the rest, Paul. It's you he wants. It's in the bag, take it from me. You're a winner, Paul. Anyway, it's time you got out of that den of losers.'

That evening Mary rang. Another present through the post.

A cat's paw this time, with another photo of the increasingly mutilated Sambo fast disappearing under a blanket of bandages.

'Do something!' she said. 'Anything they want. Just get them to stop this.'

33

Pam stood over him, hands on hips. Accusing.

'You can't take it!' she said.

Paul had enough to think about without this.

'Might,' he said, just to annoy her.

'You shit!'

'If I'm the best, why not?'

She was angry now. 'Because you just can't.'

'Why not?'

'Because . . . because it's not right, that's why not.'

Why did he bother telling her. But he had, and he was sorry. He was troubled already and she didn't make things any easier. As usual, she hit the nail on the head. It was the way it was done: underhand, unfair. Nasty. But it was what came next that really threw him.

'Anyway, who says you're the best?'

'What?'

'Think about it.'

'Think about what?'

'Johnson, right? According to your girlfriend.'

'Look, she's not . . .'

'And who was trying to get you shifted off Runian's site for so long?'

She saw him pause.

'Click?' she said. 'And why would someone who thought you such an arse suddenly realise he can't live without you – and wants to promote you?'

She watched his mind working.

'Click?' she encouraged again.

But there was fight in him yet. 'No, that's just where you're wrong, smart-aleck.' He was getting annoyed with this. 'It was Joan suggested the job in the first place. Nothing to do with Johnson, see. Joan. So there!'

She drew back to observe him from a distance, as if inspecting him for the first time. She shook her head sadly.

'Haven't a clue, have you?'

'About what?'

She paused. 'Johnson and your beloved Joan.'

'What about them?'

She paused again. 'Never guessed, did you?'

'What?'

She paused again.

He was really irritated now. 'What?'

She tried to break it to him gently. 'They're shaggin each other stupid.'

He smiled. She'd say anything, that one.

'Don't believe me, do you?'

'Would I doubt you?'

'I'm telling you. I friggin saw them.'

An uneasy feeling began in his stomach.

'Rubbish!'

'Truth hurts, eh?'

'Johnson and Joan!'

He laughed. But it was a nervous laugh. He couldn't believe it. He wouldn't believe it. The man was old enough to be her father – the dirty brute. Almost as old as himself in fact! Yet he'd seen them together in the restaurant. And she was always up seeing him in his office. No. Impossible. He dismissed the idea. Pam would say anything to shock. A woman scorned.

'And how d'you know this?'

'Saw them eatin the faces off each other in the boardroom.'

'You're having me on.'

'I swear!'

'Look, Pam – '

'Then having a shower together. Real romantic.'

The detail seemed to bring it to life. The doubt he thought he'd banished slunk back again. He looked her straight in the eyes.

'You're kidding me, right?'

'Paul, I swear. I friggin saw them.'

She meant it.

He sat back. The doubt wasn't slinking any more; it was elbowing its way cursing and shouting, into his brain. A picture began to form. And then, slowly, the bigger picture behind that one.

Just in case he'd missed one or two nuances, she helped him out.

'They're using you, you dick!'

He said nothing. There was nothing to say.

'Y'see it now? They want to kick you upstairs. You're causing too much trouble on that stupid site of yours. Maybe even costing Johnson his directorship. And they can't get rid of you any other way. They've used you, her and him both. You absolute dick!'

Next day he started making enquiries. Seems it was common knowledge that Joan was Johnson's latest conquest. Not, apparently, that there was much conquering entailed. She was ambitious to get to the top; he was a ladder. She mounted him and he returned the favour. They used each other. And now they had both tried to use him.

The first one he told about withdrawing his job application was Tony. He gripped his arm.

'Wasted you would've been.'

'Wasn't ever that fussy, really.'

'You're an architect – not a clerk!' Tony hesitated, then looked around. His voice dropped. 'Heard you were out on one of my sites a while back?'

Paul felt like a thief caught in the act.

'Ah . . . yes. Just to see different approaches. Don't mind, do you?'

Tony looked up. 'Not my best, that.'

'Looked OK,' Paul lied.

Tony dropped his eyes again. 'The things you're up against! Sometimes you get worn down. Sometimes you've to turn a blind eye if you want to get anything done. Know what I'm saying?'

Paul was hearing his confession.

Tony looked him straight in the eye. 'Don't let it happen to you, Paul. Don't let them castrate you!'

Paul looked at him. Tony was ten years older. He saw himself in ten years' time. He felt a sharp pain between his legs.

The two policemen blocked out the daylight, jamming their shoulders in the hall doorway.

'Seeing a lot of you, aren't we, sir?'

Paul blinked. It was the same two.

Since Mary's latest surprise in the post, the police had become more active. A local paper had started running the story about the psycho going around cutting up moggies. No cat was safe. People were outraged. Public representatives took up the clamour and pressure was applied. Sambo wasn't a joke any more. Sambo was a story. Sambo was hot. One paper even found a novel angle: CATHOLIC CAT VICTIM OF BUTCHER GANG.

'Caught that sicko yet?' Paul added his bit to the pressure.

'The cat? Not yet, sir. I'm afraid there's been a . . . paws . . . in our investigation.'

He smiled.

Paul didn't.

'No, it's not the cat, sir,' said the thin one. He looked at Paul. 'Does the name Mary mean anything to you?'

Paul's mouth started to open.

'No, not your wife, sir. Joseph Mary Corrigan to be precise, known to some of his associates, behind his back like, as "Mary". Seems his parents were very religious.'

Paul shook his head.

'He knows you. Says he works on your building site.'

Paul shrugged. 'Who is he? What is he?'

'A brickie, he says.'

'Dozens of them there. Look, what's this about, anyway?'

'We're not exactly sure. But there might be a connection with the fire at your rugby club . . .'

'The club?'

'He had a membership card on his person. We suspected he wasn't the rugby-playing type.'

'Oh.'

'Yours.'

'My card!'

'Now how do you suppose he got that?'

The policeman looked at him. Surely they didn't think he'd any connection with the fire.

'He must be the one stole my jacket and wallet. I reported it. Where did you find him?'

'He was about to practise micro-surgery on a man's knee-caps, with a Black and Decker drill and a lump hammer!'

'Nice person!'

'Not nearly as nice as he sounds, sir. I suppose if I'd been called Mary I'd have turned out funny too. Anyway, we had to let him go ...'

'What!'

'Well, as he hadn't actually started his operation, and as he said the tools were for some DIY job, and as he said he just found your card on the ground, and as the victim didn't want to make a complaint, we just had to let him go. But we're going to be watching him.'

'The thing is,' said the thin, sharp one, 'we reckon all this is connected somehow back to your building site. A lot of funny goings-on there. Know any reason why?'

He shook his head. If he told them what he really thought – that a few leg breakers were dictating the progress of mass housing development in a major city – they'd think he was mad. Or, even worse, that he wasn't!

They left.

Paul thought he saw the doctor smile as he beckoned him in. A change; bedside manner obviously improving. Must be taking classes.

He was wrong.

'Still alive, Mr Fox?'

The smile was really a grimace.

The check-up was as brief as before.

'Living like an evil bastard, are you?'

'Sort of.'

'Not bottling things up?'

'Not really.'

'Not really! Not really! You have to be positive, man. Look at me ... I'm positive about everything and I've the blood pressure of an Olympic athlete!'

It was nice he had something going for him, particularly when he lacked so many other attributes: height, good build, good teeth, hair.

'Any side effects from the tablets?'

'None I've noticed.' He didn't mention his dizzy spells. They came and went so quickly.

'Well, we don't seem to have shifted this pressure much. Tell you what – ' he started to write – 'we'll try something a bit stronger. That should do the trick.'

'I was hoping I could cut them down.'

'You've no side effects?'

'No.'

'So?'

'It's just . . . I've never taken tablets. For anything. It's just the idea of them. I was hoping I could come off them sometime.'

He looked at Paul.

'Mr Fox, you don't seem to understand. These are helping you. These are your friends – for life.'

Sounded just like a marriage. Except for the friends bit.

The news that Paul wasn't taking the job, wasn't moving from the office, wasn't leaving his site supervision work, was greeted with almost universal gloom. Ken felt he was stuck with this thorn in his side. Runian, Maguire and the foreman could barely bring themselves to talk to him. Danny, sensing trouble ahead, seemed to be shaping up for yet another nervous breakdown. The brickies growled as he passed by. Only Tony and Pam had a cheery word for him. Stella said little; she wanted to be sure she was on the winning side – problem was deciding which one it was. Val just wanted everybody to be good friends.

Joan, however, dropped him like a brick.

She rang once just to check that what she heard was true.

'But why, Paul?'

'I like getting bits of my cat in the post.'

'Pardon?'

'Then maybe you don't know about that.'

'Paul, what are you talking about?'

'I suppose I'm jealous really.'

'What . . .'

'Of you.'

She laughed. Warily. 'Me?'

'You told me Brian . . . er . . . Mr Johnson liked me.'

'Well, yes, he does.'

'Really liked me, you said.'

'Of course he does.'

'Then why's he never asked me to have a shower with him in the boardroom.'

He heard the intake of breath.

'Joan?'

Click.

He felt a great sense of relief. The world looked different now. Now everything was out in the open, he felt reborn. He didn't give a damn any more: about Ken, Steve, Johnson or anybody. And particularly not Joan. Yes, he was free of her at last.

Once again he was a scourge on the site. Nothing escaped his eye. Maguire and Runian winced at his approach. And well they might. Once again the whole site seemed employed in redoing work rather than progressing.

For Runian this was soul-destroying. He felt himself going down the tubes. His overheads were increasing while his income was shrinking. After a lifetime of living on the edge, this site was finally going to pull him under. This bloody architect was going to pull him under. He was desperate. But he knew what he would do, what he had to do. He was a drowning man clutching at straws, or, in this case, barbed wire.

It was time to ask a favour of his brother-in-law.

34

'**G**eronimo!'

It seemed a long time since he'd sailed past Val's head. He just hadn't felt like it lately. The joy had gone out of his life. The flesh was willing but the spirit was weak. But today it was all change. Today he felt he was on top of things at last. He felt as if he was emerging from a mist, a dark night of the soul. He had been through the furnace and had been cleansed by the fire. Back to his old self.

But something was different. Val was different. She didn't flinch and turn her head away as usual. Didn't even notice. As if he wasn't even there. She just kept staring at the out-stretched fingers of her left hand. Suddenly she thrust them up at him.

'Look,' she squeaked, twiddling the finger on which a bunch of diamonds sparkled, 'I'm engaged ... Aaaaa-aahhhhhh!'

It was some sort of female bonding call, for instantly Pam and Stella rushed over to gather around the ring.

'Aaaaaaaahhhhhh!' screeched Stella.

'Aaaaaaaahhhhhh!' screeched Pam.

They began laughing and hugging each other.

Val engaged! Who'd have thought it! Still, takes all types. At least that was one admirer off his back. He glanced dutifully at the ring. An old saying slunk unworthily to mind: 'Made of glass, set in brass, and stamped with the heel of a navvy's boot.'

He felt like an intruder. No place for a man, this. Woman's world, all that hugging and squeaking. Tony and Ken were out on site. He headed out as well. Nobody bothered to look up when he said cheerio.

Women.

But his trip to the site wasn't just an escape. There was a message by his phone that morning saying 'somebody' from the site had rung, asking the architect to come urgently. Strange. Nobody out there ever asked him to come; they hated the sight of him. So it must be something special. The message was in Val's writing, but there was no point in asking her now in her demented state. It wasn't Danny asking; he was off sick again. And certainly not the builder; each visit cost him serious money.

An eerie silence hung over the place. It was deserted. What noise there was came from the houses the countrymen were working in. They didn't come out to greet him. Normally they were ready to banter with anyone and everyone. He went to the clerk of works' hut. No one. He went to the foreman's hut. No one. No brickies. Nobody. No machinery. Nothing.

What was going on? Who sent the message? Why wasn't the sender here? Where was everybody? He was uneasy. The silence was unnatural. He decided to make his way back to the car, but as he turned – he walked right into them. A group of hooded figures confronted him. Only a glimpse, then a blanket was thrown over his head and he was lifted off the ground, carried kicking and screaming, and bundled into a car.

'Heywhatafucksallthisabout!' he burbled through the

blanket. Rage overcame his terror.

The reply was a blow to the side of the head.

He woke up lying on the hard wooden floor of a sparsely furnished bedroom. He would have preferred the bed, but it was already occupied by three seated figures. Three others stood looking down at him. All hooded.

'Stubborn bastard, aren't you?' said one who seemed to be the leader. He had a gentle voice. Kindly even.

'Wouldn't take the hint, would you?'

The men then sat on his arms and legs, pinioning him to the floor. A gag was tied round his mouth.

'Paid no attention to the warnins, did yeh, smart arse?' The kindly one produced a Black and Decker drill and a lump hammer. 'Maybe you'll pay attention now, ay?'

Paul's undivided attention was assured.

Maybe the man was going to do some DIY improvements about the house? Could do with it. Bit of shelving maybe? Paul wanted very much to believe that. Very much.

'You'll not be walkin around too many sites after this ... Stoppin honest people makin a livin, puttin out our lights.'

The kindly one turned the drill in his hand, inspecting it, blowing dust off it, like a cowboy admiring his shooting iron. He fingered the bit. He looked close. Then closer. His face twisted with annoyance.

'Fuck's sake! Friggin masonary bit! Where's the other, the wood-borin one?'

'Sure, what's the difference, Mary?'

The kindly one spun round and thumped the speaker.

'How many times I've to tell you? No friggin names – specially that one!'

The thumped one produced another bit and the kindly one fitted it. He smiled.

'That's the job now! Chews a bigger hole.' He smiled.

And it's slower.'

Paul closed his eyes. Didn't want to think what was coming next. Nothing he could do about it. He heard the drill whirr into life. His heart raced. He felt his trouser leg being rolled up.

Just then he felt four little pressure points on his chest, exactly like a small animal moving, exactly like –

He opened his eyes.

'Sambo!'

There he was! Sambo, alive and well! Sambo complete with all eyes, ears and paws. A full working model. In rude and furry health. Tail stiffly and arrogantly erect. Was it a dream?

Sambo licked his face in recognition. The tiny coarse tongue was the friendliest thing in the room.

The hooded ones sniggered. The driller thought it hilarious.

'Thought he was a gonner, didn't you? Do wonders with negatives, these days.'

He tilted the whirring drill upwards as he enjoyed his joke.

'Found a dead cat. Did for spare parts. Fooled you all right, ay?'

Then his tone changed. He leaned down into Paul's face.

'You really thought I'd done that, didn't you, ay? Didn't you?' His eyes narrowed. 'Me! Do that to one of God's poor dumb creatures? You sick fuck!'

Paul saw the madness. He shook his head wildly.

'What you take me for, ay? Think I'm some sorta friggin psycho!'

His hand now moved slowly down and forward, aligning the spinning steel bit with the centre of Paul's kneecap.

Paul tensed himself. He felt the wind as the bit hovered just above his skin. His racing heart went into overdrive. He felt cold and sweaty. A sudden pain crushed his chest.

Then – all hell broke loose. He heard shouting, doors crashing open. Breaking furniture. A policeman's face peered down anxiously into his. But only one thing mattered: the pain.

Then . . .

Oblivion.

35

He was three days in hospital before he got a visitor.

'Been in the wars, haven't we, sir!'

The two policemen beamed down at him, one at either side of the bed. The fat one proffered a bunch of grapes, the thin one a box of Roses chocolates.

'We did laugh. That cat business.' Both chortled again to prove the point. 'You have to admit it was funny.'

Nobody enquired how he was.

'But all's well that end's well, sir,' said the fat one. 'We're keeping . . . Sambo . . . down in the barracks till you get out. We called at your wife's house, but neighbours said she's away somewhere. Holiday or something.'

A holiday – and him at death's door! Said it all, that did! But then, if she was away, how would she know? And anyway, who was she away with?

Suddenly he felt sick. He had a picture of Mary and Bigmouth lolling naked together on a Greek beach. The dirty bitch! He was angry. In twenty years of marriage she'd never done that with him. Anyway, see if he cared. It was young firm bodies he fancied – like hers was all those years ago. Not like now, a sack of spuds.

The policemen stayed just long enough to finish off the grapes, the chocolates and a glass of water the nurse brought him, then left. They were grateful for his helping them catch Mary and his gang in the act. They'd be put away for a long time.

'Though, mind you,' said the fat one, 'when all's said and done, Mary wasn't all bad. Not all bad.'

'Come again?' Paul thought he hadn't heard right.

'Sadistic murderer and torturer he might be, but he was nice to animals, I'll give him that.'

'Ah, yes,' said the thin one, 'a right big softee under it all.'

They'd suspected an attack on Paul was imminent, so they'd followed him. The operation was a great success; just a pity he'd had a heart attack in the middle of it all. He'd missed them breaking Mary's nose with batons. Nice one, that. They had a small smiling silence as they relived the moment. But you can't plan for a heart attack, the fat one wisely observed. Doctor said it was only a mild one. He was lucky the police arrived on time. Anyway, he'd be up and about and home in a week.

They were his only visitors. The days passed without any eager feet rushing to his bedside. A Get Well card signed by everyone came from the office – but no one called, not even Tony. Not a word from Joan. An unsigned card arrived – Danny, cautious as ever; the muddy finger-prints the obvious giveaway. Nothing from Mary. Then one from Pam apologising for not being able to visit as she was going off for a week to Paris with one of the country-men from the site.

That surprised him. So he wasn't her object of desire after all! He was beginning to feel a total reject. First there was Mary and Bigmouth; then the Joan revelations; then Val and her engagement; and now Pam! Everyone was pairing off – all of them except him.

Visitors came to the other beds in the ward, buzzing and chatting. But no one came for him. Even the nurses felt sorry for him. It must have been them sent the priest.

'Man is born to die . . .' the priest intoned, flopping down into the bedside chair and wearily settling into a well-rehearsed spiel.

Paul cut him short.

'None of that please, father!'

Christ's sake, he was getting out in a few days!

Seeing this wasn't a spiritual person he was dealing with, the priest changed tack. He surveyed Paul's grapeless, orangeless, sweetless cupboard.

'It's a terrible thing to be lonely at the closing of one's life,' he began, a little less confidently than before, and keeping a wary eye on the awkward customer before him.

Paul looked at him. A young man of thirty. Probably hadn't interfered with his first choirboy yet. What did he know about it? About life? About anything?

He wasn't having it.

'Father . . .'

'Yes, my son?' said the thirty-year-old to the forty-five-year-old.

'Would you ever fuck away off!'

Bad move. Even the nurses avoided him after that. Seems he was their favourite priest. He was sorry, especially since there was one nurse he really liked. Huge tits, great legs – she had everything. Getting on great with her, he was. And he had a feeling, just a feeling, that there was a bit of a spark there. His confidence survived even her having to change his bedpan. But now he'd blown it. Now they all thought he was a weirdo. Only essential medical contact was maintained.

Time dragged. He tried to get out of bed but he was so weak he just fell backwards. The nurses helped him back in, like an old man. So this is what his life had become! Where were all his so-called friends? Where were the rugby club people? Where was Tony? Where was Ken? Where was Pam? Val? Or Mary, especially Mary, his friggin ex-(almost) wife of twenty years? Surely that must mean something.

He knew the answer, of course: they were all getting on with their own lives. Nobody gave a bugger about him. He'd told a few home truths and they hadn't liked to hear them. So what? He wasn't holding anything back any more. Much healthier this way – so the doctor had said.

But was it? When that had been said he wasn't in an intensive care ward, like now. Strange how stressed you could be even when not bottling things up. Looking back, he could see that in attempting to do the right thing he had managed to bring a whirlwind of tension and strife to whatever he touched. He was anything but healthy. He was supposed to be leaving in a few days, but he didn't feel like a well man. 'Nice to get home,' the nurse had said. But he wasn't going home. He was going to a flat without companionship, without intelligent conversation – a cold, cheerless, lonely flat with only Sambo for company. And there couldn't be much intelligent conversation with him – just small talk mostly.

It was visiting time again. Despair settled on him. His daily humiliation was about to begin. His exposure. His Via Dolorosa. A man who'd walked this earth for forty-five years and didn't have a friend to visit him when he was sick. What a saddo! In the distance he heard the hurrying feet and the excited chatter as visitors gushed into the ward, faces seeking eagerly for their stricken loved ones. They settled around them, parcels of fruit, sweets, drinks being opened. His bed alone was a fruit-free, sweet-free, drink-free area: an oasis of stillness in the buzzing ward. Christmas was only a few days away now, and the decorations festooning the ward only added to his gloom. There would be no happy Christmas for him.

That morning he got a fright. A nurse was helping him to the toilet when he caught a glimpse of himself in the glass door of an unlit room. An old man looked back at him. He looked again. Was that really him? No way. In his mind, he was always a trim mid-thirties with the body of a Greek god and the suave, evil-bastard features of Richard Gere. People often remarked that he never looked his age. But now this reflection was his Dorian Gray attic; from it an ashen-faced old man stared back at him, looking every inch of sixty, plus time added on for bad behaviour.

'Paul! What's happened you?'

The voice woke him from his reverie. He opened his eyes. Looked. Blinked. It was all wrong: the appearance, the warmth, the concern. It was all wrong – but it was her all right.

'Mary!'

She lunged forward, grabbing with open arms for his head and shoulders.

He flinched. An attack. Then the kisses planted on his head called for a reassessment. But this wasn't the Mary he knew. Christ, she was even crying!

'What's wrong with you?' he said.

She looked amazed. 'Me?'

'Look at you! Blubbing!'

'What do you think! I'm worried about you.'

'About me?'

He was getting out in a few days!

'You, y'eejit!'

OK, he'd had a heart attack. A mild one. Nothing much to it, the doctor said. A man like him, the doctor said, an athlete – sure, a thing like that was no bother to him! Said he'd never seen a man with such a strong constitution. Stood to him.

'So what's all this fuss, then?'

'Of course I'm worried about you! Only natural.'

He looked at her. He felt a flutter of panic. She meant it.

Did she know something he didn't? Oh, Jesus, he must be on his way out!

'When they said you'd had a heart attack, I just couldn't believe it!'

She pulled back and looked at him.

'I thought, I thought you might be . . . dead!'

The four-letter word shocked him. He checked hurriedly around. It wasn't a word for hospital precincts. It was like shouting 'Christmas' on a turkey farm. Anyway, the absurdity of the remark put him at ease. He relaxed and inspected her.

He was surprised at what he saw. If he'd met her on the street, he could have passed by. She was quite different. She was, well, younger-looking. Amidst the pasty-faced inhabitants of the ward, she was a picture of health. She was tanned. She was trim and fit-looking, in a smart two-piece suit. She was totally transformed without her trademark soiled T-shirt and tracksuit bottoms. He couldn't remember when he last saw her in something other. And she was wearing make-up.

'What you looking at?' She felt uneasy at his stare.

'Nothing.'

But he was. He was looking at a different Mary. Or he was looking at her in a different way.

And she was looking at him. She sighed. 'Suppose I'll have to take you back now.'

'What?'

'On parole of course.'

He didn't know what to say. Didn't know whether to be annoyed or grateful.

'You can't live on your own in that hovel after this. Have sense! You need looking after.'

She had a point. But he'd play hard to get.

'And what if I don't want to come back?'

'Suit yourself. Have you another option?'

He hadn't. Game over.

'Y'know, when I heard – ' she looked at her watch – 'just an hour ago, I thought . . . I thought . . .'

'The insurance policy?'

'Shut up!'

'Just a joke.'

'I thought . . . what if he dies? I thought . . . I'll miss him, bastard and all that he is.'

'That's nice.'

A tear came into her eye.

'I thought . . . twenty years must mean something. We've had our ups and downs. We know each other through and through . . .' She was crying freely now. 'We're not getting any younger. We're both facing into middle age. I don't want to do it alone. Nobody does. Do you?'

He felt his own eyes moisten. Steady on. He didn't really want to get into this emotional bath with her. But she was right. He was on his own. Where were all his erstwhile friends? Only Mary had come to see him. When the chips were down, only she could be relied on. He knew what he wanted: a companion. And sex. But companionship most of all. He was wearying of fickle younger women. Exciting, yes, but he couldn't have a proper intelligent conversation with them. And anyway, where were they now?

But still he held back. He could see all the practical reasons for returning. But it would be on her terms. It would be an end to his freedom, an end to acting the lad, an end to the thrill of the chase; it would be an end to his pretending that he wasn't married to a forty-five-year-old woman. It would be an acceptance that he was one half of a settled middle-aged couple. And that's what, most of all, he couldn't stand, for it was the beginning of the end. He wanted to hold at bay that final acknowledgement, that long slow decline, that slipping unnoticed into old age, anonymity and irrelevance.

But now his heart attack had changed all that. It was nature's way of telling him he was fucked; telling him to grow up, that things die off, that old age is inevitable; and so, unbelievably, is death. Indeed, he could consider himself lucky. Poor Rory had been only thirty-five. No warning for him. One last asparagus supper and he was off to vegetate for ever in that great organic meadow in the sky.

He hated dwelling on such things. A stab of jealousy made him change tack.

'How was your holiday with Bigmouth?'

'Pardon?'

'Heard you were away.'

'I was. Staying with my sister in Dublin for a week. Couldn't stand being alone in the house ...'

So no frolicking on the beach.

'And what's this about Jim?'

'Thought you and he – '

'Haven't seen him for weeks. And that's not long enough. Why you asking?'

'Nothing.'

She looked at him. Then started to smile. 'God ... I believe you're jealous! You are. You're bloody jealous!'

'Me!'

'So that's what's behind all this! You eejit! Jim's a good heart, but he must be the most boring man on the planet. He even bored the cat. I think it volunteered to be kidnapped.' She started to laugh. 'You eejit'. She launched herself at him again, hugging him, clutching him tight.

To his surprise, he found himself returning the embrace. It felt natural. He realised how much he'd missed this, this simple token of human comfort; indeed – once he allowed himself to think about it – how much he had missed her, herself. Now he felt at home. He had returned to the womb.

Maybe this was how it should be: the unexciting but cosy familiarity of a twenty-year marriage. He'd found that the life of a forty-five-year-old single male wasn't so enticing after all. Maybe he should content himself. Maybe this is as good as it gets. The regular meals, the slippers by the fire, the indifferent annual sex. He pulled her closer, resigning himself to his fate. From now on he must make the best of what he had.

'I do love you, you bastard,' she mumbled in his ear.

'I love you too,' he said.

And he meant it. And it shocked him that he meant it. It had always been there, he realised that now. But he'd been bottling it up. He saw now what a fool he'd been. He was suddenly filled with remorse, ashamed of the feelings now sweeping over him. Ashamed to admit that Mary's ageing face was a daily reminder of his own advancing years, his own mortality. Now, after a heart attack, no other reminder was necessary. Ashamed to admit that he needed younger women to reinforce the youthful vision he had of himself. Ashamed to admit to his genuine love for his wife, bottling it up, refusing to let it out; refusing to grow old like her; refusing to grow old with her. Refusing to grow.

And he meant it too when he said, with a resigned sigh, that his chasing days were over. 'I've been stupid. Risking losing you. Risking losing everything.' Maybe he would have a happy Christmas after all.

She burst out crying again.

'You really mean it?' she said. 'Really, really mean it?'

Just then, over her shaking shoulder, he saw the nurse with the huge tits and the long legs. She smiled over at him. Yes, there was definitely something there.

He winked.

She winked back.

'Of course I do,' he said.